Screenshot

ALSO BY DONNA COONER

Skinny
Can't Look Away
Worthy

Screenshot

DONNA COONER

POINT

TO KATY,
A BRILLIANT WRITER AND EVEN BETTER FRIEND

ISBN 978-1-338-33987-1

10 9 8 7 6 5 4 3 2 1   18 19 20 21 22

Printed in the U.S.A.   23

First printing 2018

Book design by Yaffa Jaskoll

One of the first descriptions of a social network was a series of memos by J. C. R. Licklider in 1962. He called it the Galactic Network.

Early creators of the internet called themselves Internauts.

CHAPTER ONE

SKYE

The man in front of me has three dead goldfish in a Ziploc baggie. He's wearing a camouflage T-shirt that doesn't quite cover his stomach and he's peering at me over the top of a pair of hot-pink reading glasses, as though I can solve the problem in the bag.

I can't. I just work here.

"The sign says 'Customer Satisfaction Always,' right?" he asks. "I bought them on Wednesday morning and they were like this on Thursday night."

Well, not quite like *that*. "Are they frozen?" I ask.

He nods. "I put them in the freezer. I wanted to preserve them until I could come back in the store."

Let's just get this over with. I ask, "Do you have a receipt?"

"No. But they cost $4.68 each. They were on sale."

"So, $14.04 total," I say, plugging the number into the service desk refund register.

"Did you do that in your head?" he asks, blinking at me.

"Yep," I say.

"Are you some kind of child genius?"

"I'm sixteen. Not exactly a child." I carefully pick up the baggie with just my finger and thumb. "And yes, I'm a genius."

Because that's why I'm working here at the Kmart returns desk.

He doesn't get my sarcasm. He smiles, embarrassed by the tears in his eyes over those dead fish. There is no ring on his stubby finger, so maybe the fish are all the company he has, and instantly I feel guilty. *At least you could get a cat or something. I think we sell hamsters. Get a hamster. Something with fur.*

"Sign here," I say, pushing the return slip across the counter. I smile back at him, and that seems to improve his mood.

"Smile more" is the first thing on my new to-do list. See, I was elected student council vice president this past fall, but next year I want to run for student council president. And just last week, I read online about how important "likability" is in a candidate. But likability is such an intangible quality. What does it even mean? So I did some research. Okay, I did a *lot* of research. And "smiling more" seemed to be a key ingredient. If I ever want to run for *real* office someday, I need to learn this kind of stuff now. I've always been a hard worker.

"Thanks," the fish guy says, signing the slip.

I notice that the assistant manager, Mr. King, is watching us from over by the magazine racks. Mr. King is only the part-time assistant manager. The rest of the time he is the faux barista and works at the store's snack bar. He is tall and thin, all elbows and Adam's apple, and he mostly smells like lettuce with a whiff of coffee when he twirls around, which he does a lot.

Who knew lettuce had a smell?

Despite his smell, Mr. King is not a bad guy as managers go. On slow late nights, he used to make extra frozen lattes and pour them into tiny little plastic cups. He'd put them out on a plastic clearance Valentine's Day heart-shaped tray and say they were samples, but he gave most of them to his staff. Until a cashier told him that was practically stealing. Mr. King is super active in the New Life Baptist Church. So I no longer get free caffeine samples and Mr. King has to pray a little extra for his generosity.

Thou shalt not give away too many samples of Frappuccinos. I Venti 3:14

I give Mr. King a confident little nod, to tell him I'm on top of this whole dead fish thing, but he just walks off toward Toys. I figure I'm definitely a contender for employee of the month.

"I'm very sorry for your loss," I tell the man across the counter. He gives a big sniff and pushes the pink reading glasses up his nose. I hand him his money back and say, "Have a nice day."

I'm supposed to say that after every transaction. I'm good at doing what's expected—it's my superpower. Sometimes people are good because they want to be good, and sometimes it's just because they are afraid of NOT being good. I probably fall into the second group.

After the fish guy leaves, I glance down at my phone under the counter. This is against the rules, but Mr. King isn't close by.

I open ChitChat, everyone's current social media obsession. The thing that makes ChitChat different from other apps is that you can't set your profile to private. Whatever you post is up there for all the world to see—unless you choose to delete it, of course. But the other catch? You can't delete any posts until fifteen minutes have passed. No takedowns, no edits. My best friend, Asha, says it makes you commit to what you post. I think she just loves the edginess of it all. Sort of like truth *and* dare all rolled into one.

I go to Asha's profile. All her posts include her signature hashtag: #IAmAshaMirza. Like people wouldn't know?

#IAmAshaMirza *running*.

#IAmAshaMirza *at my locker*.

#IAmAshaMirza *snowboarding*.

The latest is a video, posted right after school today. It's captioned #IAmAshaMirza *eating a taco*. And, if you had any doubts, she is taking a big bite. Over and over again. On an endless ChitChat loop.

Seriously?

Of course, I am quick to notice the undeniable differences between our lives. Because that is what the internet is for, right?

First of all, Asha's *not* standing under fluorescent lights in an ugly blue smock, next to a stack of too-tight jeans, a pile of sales flyers, and a Ziploc baggie full of three dead goldfish. She *is* wearing sunglasses and there is a lake sparkling behind her. Not just any lake—it's the lake she actually lives on. The wind blows her thick black hair off her face to one side, like those photos with models in front of fans. Only this is real. *Or at least as real as Asha gets.* Her short-sleeved shirt is pink with flowers and shows off her sculpted arms to perfection. Considering it's March in Colorado, she has to be freezing in that shirt. But it does look good on her. She smiles at the camera in that "I know I'm hot, but if you tell me that in a disrespectful manner, I will beat you to a pulp" kind of way.

I imagine posting a selfie—me in my sad blue smock, standing behind the service desk.

#IamSkyeMatthews *stuck at work.*

I smirk. No way. Asha would be furious if I stole her signature line. Besides, ChitChat is all about showing off.

I close out of ChitChat and check my email. I have one hope of escaping the Kmart service desk this summer. Her name is Senator Ann Watson. She is the youngest member of the United States Congress, and her Colorado office is located right here in town. If she would just read my outstanding application answer to *Why You Should Be Our Summer Intern*, I'm sure I'd get a response.

But there is no email from the congresswoman or her staff. I sigh. Things could be worse. I could have only dead fish for friends.

Since I have a phone in my hand and haven't been caught yet, I pull up a picture of me, Asha, and our other best friend, Emma. The Three Musketeers. We've been together since we were ten. We couldn't be more different—inside and out. Asha is short and powerful, with brown skin, jet-black hair that frames her heart-shaped face, and bright-green eyes. The leader of our little group, she loves to do things other people are afraid of. She loves it even more if she can make someone else do these things with her.

Emma is pale, blonde, tall, and willowy. She can recite a hundred movie scenes from memory, but can't remember her homework. A little spacey maybe, but she's the heart of our group. I don't know who Emma would pick if she had to choose between me and Asha. I don't ever want to find out.

Then there's me in the middle, where I always seem to end up. The mediator. The politician. I have long, light-brown hair and hazel eyes. I'm ordinary. Not striking like my best friends are.

I decorate our faces on the screen with some silly filters and balloon emojis. Then I text the photo to Asha.

ME: HAPPY BIRTHDAY!

She answers immediately.

ASHA: THANKS. ANY BLUE LIGHT SPECIALS?
ME: HA. VERY FUNNY.

From someone who has never had to work even a part-time job in her life.

ME: HOW WAS YOUR TACO? ☺
ASHA: DELISH. WORKED IT OFF. JUST RAN 15
MILES AND READY FOR BDAY CAKE NOW!

Asha is training for a marathon. One of these days, I have no doubt she's going to lead some elite special operation to rescue hostages from a dangerous dictator.

Then I remember. *Oh, no. The cake.*

I text my boyfriend, Luke.

ME: CAKE?
LUKE: ALMOST DONE. MAKING GANACHE
FROSTING. WILL BRING IT WHEN I PICK
YOU UP.

Luke and I are the perfect couple. He likes to cook all the things. I like to eat all the things. Luke is also adorable, with curly dirty-blond hair, bright blue eyes, and a soccer-star body. He's my first real boyfriend. The first guy who ever kissed me in the school hallway—outside the band classroom on September 9. The first guy I ever went to a big dance with—the winter prom, January 27. The first guy everyone linked my name with—Luke and Skye. It has a nice ring to it.

Everyone says so.

I glance over my shoulder at the clock on the wall behind me. Two hours and thirty-two more minutes of price checks and broken blenders before Luke picks me up and drives me to Asha's for her birthday sleepover.

I've been looking forward to *and* dreading this Friday. It will be great to see my best friends, of course. But I'm worried our conversation will eventually turn to all the fun summer plans in the works. If Senator Watson doesn't respond to my application soon, my summer is definitely not going to be fun.

I slide my phone into my pocket. *Back to work.*

I watch as a customer in the toothbrush aisle selects a purple one from the top row. She pushes her loaded shopping cart with one squeaky, broken wheel toward the checkout. Harmony Heaven is the only cashier we have on duty right now. With a name like Harmony Heaven, she should be nice.

She is not.

Harmony is built like a brick wall, tall and formidable. She's white, with wide blue eyes and a mouth always set in a scowl. This week her hair is fried blonde on the ends and dark brown at the roots. Last week it was entirely purple. The top of my head comes up to Harmony's armpit. I'm curvy—some people might even call me fat—but Harmony is solid. No one would ever call her fat. At least not to her face.

Harmony takes each individual item out of the shopping cart. She glares at the customer, a woman in Lululemon yoga pants and a CrossFit hoodie, as though she has committed the greatest sin on the planet by simply wanting to buy a toothbrush.

"Hey." I can hear Harmony yelling at me from the number three counter, but I keep my head down, thinking maybe Mr. King will walk by and have to answer. He doesn't, and Harmony just gets louder.

"Hey, Boss Girl," she yells. Harmony likes to call me that even though she knows my name and I'm not the boss. "I need a price check on this toothbrush. She says they're on sale."

Harmony is a year older than me, but I never really noticed her much at school before we started working together. I'm not sure she's even *at* school all that often.

I look at the flyer in front of me and shout back, "Five dollars and nine cents for two of them."

Harmony doesn't respond, but I know she heard me because now she's bagging up the toothbrush. The customer gathers up her purchases and practically sprints out the front door. Nobody sticks around long to chat with Harmony.

Mr. King is still nowhere in sight, so I pull out my phone again and text Asha back.

ME: DON'T WORRY. THERE WILL BE CAKE.

ASHA: AND CANDLES?

Seriously? Nothing is ever enough for you. Of course I'd never say that to her. I start to send her a pile of poop emojis to tell her exactly how amusing she is, but then I'm interrupted.

"You better put that away."

I almost drop my phone. "Oh, God, Ryan. You scared me." I clutch my hand to my chest to stop my heart from pounding.

Ryan de la Cruz is one year ahead of me at school. He moved to Colorado from California this fall and has only been at Kmart for a couple of months. Ryan restocks shelves and usually works in the back, in Receiving. He has broad shoulders, high cheekbones, brown skin, and thick black hair. I know that both Jeanette in Women's Clothing and Bridget in Paint and Hardware think he's a "dreamboat" (their word). Even though they are both probably old enough to be his grandmothers.

Now Ryan stands before me, holding the hand of a little girl who is grinning widely and wearing several red clearance stickers on the front of her sweater.

"I need the intercom," Ryan says, nodding to the girl. I pick up the phone and key in the number for the loud-speaker before handing the phone to Ryan.

"Attention, shoppers," Ryan says, his voice echoing through the store. "We have a young lady here at our service desk, and evidently her father is lost. If you see a black-haired man named Desmond wearing a Denver Broncos T-shirt, please bring him to the service desk. His daughter is waiting for him."

Ryan looks down at the girl and she nods confidently up at him.

"That should do it," she says.

I can't help but grin at this exchange. A few minutes later, a man matching Ryan's description appears at the service desk and whisks the girl off, thanking Ryan over his shoulder.

"That was nice of you," I tell Ryan. I'm still holding my cell phone and he glances at it.

"What if I were Mr. King?" he asks, shaking his head with a small smirk. "Skye Matthews's perfect reputation would have its first black mark."

I roll my eyes at him.

"I'm not perfect," I say. But I get a small thrill out of hearing that I *seem* that way.

"True," Ryan says, looking thoughtful. Then he turns and heads back down the aisle.

I text Asha back: **SORRY, AM AT WORK. SEE YOU SOON.** I stuff the phone into the back pocket of my jeans, where I won't be as easily tempted to respond to any more texts.

I never want to be one of those girls who has to have a boyfriend to *be* someone. And I'm *not* that girl. I just like myself better when I'm filtered through Luke's eyes. His popularity is contagious. Everything is easier with him. Walking into a school cafeteria is easier. Going to class is easier. Even standing outside Kmart in the cool night air is easier, because soon Luke will be here to whisk me away.

When he pulls up, cake sitting carefully on the back seat of his Nissan Altima, I can't help but feel that familiar shiver of pride. I slide into the passenger seat and lean over the console to give him a quick kiss on the lips. Then I look out of the corner of my eye to see Harmony, Ryan, and everybody else walking past Luke's car to employee parking. I kind of hope they can see us. Let them be impressed by Skye's cute boyfriend.

"Everything okay?" Luke asks.

I glance at him, smiling at the white flour handprints on the front of his blue soccer jersey.

"Definitely better now," I say, buckling my seat belt.

As Luke drives off, I throw a shopping bag in the back seat.

"What's that?"

"I bought you a shirt," I say. "It was on clearance."

"*What?*"

Ha. I knew that would get him. Luke refuses to even set foot in Kmart. Definitely not his style. "Calm down. I'm only kidding. It's a gift card for Asha and candles for the cake."

Luke shudders. "I don't know why you don't just quit that place."

I shrug. "It's a job. I need the money."

We've had this conversation before. Many. Times.

"My dad could use another receptionist at his office in the afternoons. Then you wouldn't have to work weekends or nights," Luke says. "I could talk to him?"

I shake my head. Luke's dad is a dentist. I don't want to deal with the sound of dental drills whining and people calling to complain about their molars. I'd rather stick with what I know at Kmart.

I have big plans and am willing to work hard to make them happen.

"Thanks, but I'm going to get this internship," I say, hoping saying it will make it so.

Luke nods, but he doesn't seem very enthusiastic.

I feel a twinge of irritation. I don't say anything, though. Luke and I have been together since the start of our junior year, and things between us were great in the beginning. But ever since the winter prom in January, something small in our relationship has shifted. I can't deny that I feel the slightest distance from him now.

I push the thought away. I pull my phone out and lean across the console to film a ChitChat video of the two of us.

"Sing 'Happy Birthday' to Asha," I tell Luke, and we ham it up at the stoplight, singing loudly. The light turns green and Luke's attention goes back to driving.

I caption the video #happybirthdayAsha and post it to ChitChat. It gets a few likes right away, and I rewatch it. My hair looks weird and I wish I could reshoot it, but that's not how ChitChat works. *No takebacks.*

ASHA

Asha holds up her phone and shoots a video of herself wearing a silly striped paper hat and blowing a party horn. Then she captions it #IAmAshaMirza *celebrating*, and posts it to ChitChat. It instantly starts garnering likes and complimentary comments.

Asha leans back against the teak deck chair and sighs, scrolling through her ChitChat feed. A ton of posts bear the hashtag #happybirthdayAsha. Birthday texts from friends and acquaintances keep popping up on her screen, but she ignores them all for now.

After coming home from school and changing, she went for a good, hard run, which was helpful. Running is the only thing that shuts down her overactive mind. But her calm state is quickly disappearing.

The air by the lake has a touch of the Colorado spring snowstorm that forecasters claim will blow in over the mountains tonight. For now, though, it isn't even cold enough for a thick sweater. She unzips the Nike hoodie she wore over her black running tank top. The late afternoon sun feels pleasantly warm, even though the glare makes her squint. The world narrows into the window of her phone screen, framed by her thick, spiky lashes.

A silly sophomore, Alicia Montoya, just posted a video giving a shout-out to her new bangs. It definitely requires a response. Thank goodness ChitChat comments are anonymous. Just one more reason to love it.

DEFINITELY NOT YOUR BEST LOOK! #stylefail

While she's at it, Asha writes #stylefail under a few other posts—Beth Hunt's picture of her new Miu Miu super-round sunglasses and Jessica Martin's full-body shot in a new maxi dress. Then Asha has to make a couple of positive comments to balance things out.

One under a video of her newest crush, Nate, hiking . . .

STOP BEING SO CUTE!

And one under Emma's montage of birthday clips from random movies, captioned #HappybirthdayAsha . . .

YOU'RE THE BEST! GET OVER HERE RIGHT NOW.

Asha closes out of ChitChat and checks her texts from Skye. Asha's been kind of annoyed with Skye lately. She's always so holier-than-thou about her stupid job. It makes Asha nuts. And maybe a little jealous. It's not just the time Skye spends at work, it's the fact that she's always talking about *needing* to work. Like that some-how makes her better than everyone who doesn't. And then of course the way she's all geared up for her future political career. It can be a bit much.

Asha takes a deep breath. She crosses her arms over her chest and tucks her phone into her hoodie pocket, staring down at her lime-green Reebok running shoes.

"Honey, can you give me a hand?"

Asha turns around. Through the large sliding glass doors of the house, Asha sees her mom stringing a *Happy Birthday* banner across the wall. The table below is covered with party hats and streamers even though there will only be two guests—Emma and Skye. Asha's mom doesn't understand why she doesn't want a big birthday party.

Not this year.

"You're going to have dinner with us upstairs before your friends arrive, right?" Asha's mom calls out the door.

Asha frowns. "Yes," she says, for the third time this afternoon.

"What time are they coming?"

"Around nine."

Her mother steps out on the deck with a birthday hat in her hands. For a moment she stands looking out at the water; then her eyes drop to the hat in her hands. Her forehead wrinkles in confusion. "Is it someone's birthday?"

"Mine," Asha answers.

"Sorry," her mom says. Sadness engulfs her face. "I forgot."

"It's okay, Mom," Asha says. "Everybody forgets sometimes."

Her face clears in relief. "You're going to have dinner with us upstairs before your friends arrive, right?"

CHAPTER TWO

SKYE

Luke drops me in front of Asha's house. Her exclusive lakeside neighborhood is a beautiful hangout any time of the year. Summer is the prime time, though. Asha, Emma, and I have spent many a day paddleboarding and swimming out on that water.

Tonight, no one's on the lake; there are only geese honking as they fly in low over my head. Summer seems a long time away. The forecast must have been right for once because the air is cold now and there is no sign of the moon or stars. It even smells like snow.

Shivering, I button my coat. Then I reach back into the car to grab my overnight tote, the cake box, and the shopping bag from Luke's back seat.

"Thanks for the ride. I'll see you tomorrow night," I say to Luke.

"Have fun," he says, leaning over to give me a quick kiss.

I shut the car door, balancing the cake box in one hand,

and head around the side of the house to Asha's private downstairs entrance.

The lights from the other houses shimmer across the surface of the lake. The *real* view is only evident once you're inside one of the mansions. From Asha's giant picture windows, you can see the Rocky Mountains, and if you catch the light just right when the sun is going down, there is a perfectly mirrored reflection of mountains and sky. That's why the residents of Linden Lake pay the big bucks.

I don't come from this part of town, even though Asha and I have gone to the same public schools ever since kindergarten. I live in a house in the cheap seats, farther north, with a view of the eastern plains toward Kansas and a Budweiser plant. If I look in that direction, with my face toward the early morning sun, there are no mountains. No lakes. Just fields full of sunflowers and pumpkins in the fall and dirt in the winter.

I got over feeling intimidated by the difference in our economic statuses, long ago. Asha's parents are rich. Her whole family is rich. Her paternal grandparents, who immigrated from India, were big-shot scientists who invented a medical device that became important for saving lives when people had open-heart surgery. And her maternal grandparents, who hailed from Ireland, started a law firm. So Asha's "bedroom" is really an entire ground-floor apartment with a view of the mountains reflected in the lake. We could hang out in *my* bedroom, but there is hardly enough room for the bed. We're never invited to Emma's house. I'm not sure why. She lives partway between me and Asha. But who wants to go anywhere else when there is this place?

I knock, but it's only a courtesy, so I walk right in.

Emma is already there, sitting on the bright-red couch and watching a black-and-white movie on her iPad, her earbuds in. Her thick blonde bangs are clipped back away from her face and the rest of her hair is in a low pony. Her face is clear of makeup. She is wearing faux fur slippers, red plaid sweatpants, and a gray oversized tee that reads *Dance like no one is watching.*

The annoying thing is, Emma can wear whatever she wants and she still looks beautiful. She has this bohemian, hippie vibe going on with her long flowing hair, even though I know her monthly highlights don't come cheap. She's obsessed with movies, and I can totally see her being a famous actress someday.

Behind her, the lake glimmers in the lights from the large wraparound deck. A fire is flickering in Asha's gas fireplace, and Jura, Asha's large yellow cat, is curled up in Emma's lap. There is no sign of Asha.

Emma glances up, and I give her a big smile.

"Why are you looking at me like that?" she asks. Then she pulls out her earbuds and repeats the question like I'm the one who can't hear.

"Like what?" I ask, still smiling.

"Like this." She copies my fake grin, and her silly smile relaxes mine into a real one. I need to work on making it more natural, less fake.

"It's my *to-do* thing. I'm trying to smile more," I explain, dropping my bags on the floor and setting the cake down on the table.

"Why?" she asks.

I shrug, taking off my coat. Saying that it's part of my "likability" plan sounds a little too intense to admit out loud. "Smiling is contagious. It makes people feel better."

"Does it make *you* feel better?" she asks.

I'm not fazed. "That's not the point."

"It kind of is." She pushes one earbud into her left ear and leaves one dangling. It's her way of including me.

"Can I ask you something?" I say, and she nods. I pull my lips back from my teeth with one finger. "Do you think my teeth look any whiter?"

"I guess so. Why?"

"Tooth whitener strips. They were on sale at Kmart last week."

"How long have you been doing it?" she asks.

"Since last night."

"Oh. Totally working," she says, and gives me a thumbs-up sign.

"Thanks." I laugh.

I take off my shoes and join her on the couch, feeling the tension slip out of my shoulders as I puddle down into the warmth and soft cushions. Jura opens her eyes to a slit of green to acknowledge my presence, then closes them again. Emma doesn't put both earbuds back in, but she doesn't need the sound. She has the closed captions on because she likes to make sure she doesn't miss any of the dialogue. I don't recognize the film, but I'm sure Emma's seen it a million times before by the way she is mouthing the words along with the actors on the screen. She's on an Audrey Hepburn kick right now.

I tuck my feet up under the flannel throw. The warmth of the blanket and the fire make my eyelids droop.

Emma glances at me. "Don't start that. We have all night to party and you are *not* going to be a big old pooper."

"Sorry," I mumble. "I'll catch up. Promise. Where's the birthday girl?"

"Upstairs. Finishing family stuff." Emma crosses her long legs and chews contemplatively on a red Twizzler, her eyes never leaving the screen.

The three of us have spent every birthday together since we were ten. We only missed Emma's birthday one year, when she had her tonsils out. She was thirteen. Even then, Asha and I stayed in the hospital as long as we could for visiting hours before the nurse kicked us out.

Sometimes it's hard for me to believe we're all best

friends now. It certainly didn't start out that way. Emma, yes. Asha, no. In the fifth grade, Asha was already a born leader: always the first in class to call out the answer to a teacher's question, the first to laugh at someone else's misfortune, and definitely the first to cross any finish line ever created. Emma and I were completely intimidated. But then we were assigned to the same group for a science project in Mrs. MacLeod's class.

Asha immediately took charge. She decided we would experiment with the ideal amount of water needed to make a bean sprout grow. She assigned me the task of watering Plant One every day until it was almost dirt soup. Emma was supposed to lightly mist water on top of Plant Two every few days. And Asha herself was in charge of Plant Three. She watered it religiously every two days, no matter what. We met every Tuesday after school at Asha's house—right here—and recorded our data.

Then one day, Emma accidentally left the plants outside in subfreezing temperatures. The plants all died and the experiment was a bust. But I was the one who stepped in to keep Asha from going ballistic. I suggested we change the title of our project to "How to Fail Your Science Fair Project." It was definitely risky, so, of course, Asha loved it. We got a C, but the three of us have been inseparable ever since.

I take out my phone and check ChitChat. I must make some kind of noise because Emma asks, "What's wrong?"

"It's this girl from work. She's always posting her gym pics and stupid check-ins at random places. Like anyone cares."

I hold up my phone to show her Harmony's post from yesterday. There's a photo of a punching bag, and a "check-in" at a gym.

"I hate that," Emma says, picking up another Twizzler and refocusing on the movie. Emma isn't into working out and, for some weird reason only known to the god of genetics, she doesn't have to. "Who is she?" Emma asks.

"You don't know her. She's a senior."

"So why look at her posts?"

"Just curious." I shrug. "It's stupid. I know."

Harmony likes posting tough-girl pics. It's just about scaring people, and she's doing a good job. I'm not surprised she's a fighter. That makes her even more intimidating, but that's what makes her happy. I'll continue to keep my interactions with her to the bare minimum. Smile and nod. Don't comment. Especially not online.

"What's up, peeps?" Asha jumps down the last three steps into the center of the room. She's wearing the cute striped paper birthday hat I recognize from her earlier post on ChitChat. She's holding two more hats for me and Emma, and she hands them to us.

I stifle a yawn as Emma and I dutifully put the hats on our heads.

"I see Luke came through with the birthday cake,"

Asha says, peering into the box on the table. "Get ready to sing."

I sigh. Caffeine. I need caffeine. I notice Asha frown and I quickly plaster a smile on my face. I've seen a disappointed Asha, and no one wants that.

"You didn't want a bigger party this year?" I ask, getting up off the couch to go pull a soda out of the fridge. Last year, Asha threw a big blowout upstairs, and then we had our traditional three-person sleepover afterward.

"Yeah," Emma says. She dislodges an unhappy Jura from her lap and follows me to the fridge. "What happened to inviting a zillion people?"

Asha pulls me and Emma into a big hug. "You guys are all the people I need."

I'm not a hugger, but this one feels pretty good. There's nothing like being with your very best friends in the whole world. Asha is right. This is exactly what I needed.

I open the fridge, take out a can of soda, and take a big sip. Better. "Okay. Let's get this party started," I say.

"We need some music," Asha says, running over to her laptop. Within a few seconds, a playlist of dance music is blasting out of the speakers and we are jumping around the room like maniacs. Emma raises her long, graceful arms over her head and does a little spin, as only she can do. She smells like lavender and lemon, and in her bare feet she is still a head taller than I am. Asha grabs Emma's hands and they start a sort of weird square dance that has us all in giggles.

"Just think." Asha stretches her arms out wide like she's hugging the sky. "Only a few more months until summer vacation!"

Emma catches my eye. She is slightly out of breath. "Did you hear anything about the internship yet?" she asks me softly.

I shake my head, lifting my chin. I hate pity and I hate feeling like I put all my eggs in one very long shot of a basket. "But everyone is still probably recovering from the November elections," I tell them, hoping it's true—even though it's March.

"I know you'll hear something soon," Emma says reassuringly. "Senator Watson is going to love your application. You'll see."

I hope so. Even though it was a struggle finding the time, I spent hours helping build that Habitat for Humanity house this past summer. And then there's student council, plus the math tutoring I did in the fall. With my schedule at work, there wasn't any more I could do to make my application rise to the top.

"No worries," I say, wanting to change the subject. I raise my Diet Coke in a toast. "Tonight we celebrate Asha's seventeen trips around the sun."

"Hear, hear," Asha says, beaming. "Cake time."

We take Luke's cake out of the box. I light the candles,

like always, and Emma starts the song, like always, and we sing as loud as we possibly can. Like always. The faces in the candlelight have changed over the years, but we are all here.

I have to stop singing to clear the lump in my throat. Feeling a little silly, I blink rapidly at the emotion that rushes into my eyes. Then Asha leans over the cake to blow out the candles and the three of us are clapping and cheering.

Then we cut the cake and take pictures for ChitChat—#happybirthdayAsha—before digging into Luke's amazing chocolate creation.

"Hey, anybody want to go snowboarding tomorrow?" Asha asks, her mouth full of cake. "I'm going up to Steamboat." Her voice gets all soft and pleading. "Come on. Fresh powder."

"I'm working," I say, when I can talk through the chocolate.

She gives me a pouty face. "You're always working."

"I know," I say. "But then I'm going to Luke's house after. So that will be fun. Anyway, aren't you seeing Nate tomorrow?"

Nate is a snowboarder from Steamboat who Asha met over winter break. I've yet to meet him in real life. From what I've seen of him on ChitChat, he's a six-foot-tall, lanky white guy with blond dreadlocks who is always on academic probation. He likes to shoot gun fingers and wink at people when he talks. And he's always talking. He and Asha send each other a million videos a day. In typical Asha fashion, though, they only see each other face-to-face on occasional weekends. Long-distance, every-once-in-a-while loves are Asha's trademark.

"Yeah." Asha shrugs, studying a piece of cake on the end of her fork. "But it's better with my besties there, too." She glances hopefully at Emma.

"Nope. Can't." Emma wipes chocolate frosting off her lips with a napkin. "The Lyric Cinema is holding a screenwriting contest and I'm going there in the afternoon to hear about the deets."

"Just be that way, then. Abandon me. I'll get over it," Asha says dramatically. "And in the meantime I shall cheer myself up with presents!"

"What did you get today?" I ask.

Asha smiles widely. "My parents gave me a GNU B-Pro snowboard."

"Very cool," I say, knowing that was tops on her list.

"And anything from Nate?" Emma asks.

"No." Asha frowns, then looks at us expectantly.

That's our cue. We leave the chocolate cake behind to pull out our gifts. I reach into my Kmart shopping bag and hand Asha a gift card for iTunes so she can download her latest running playlist. She smirks when she pulls it out of the envelope.

"Thank you," she says in a singsong voice, then gives

me a hug. It would have been more thoughtful if she hadn't told me exactly what to buy her, but as usual, I didn't disappoint.

"I have some presents for you, too," Emma says, and I can't help but cringe a little. Emma gives the perfect gifts—thoughtful, unique, and beautifully wrapped. It's her thing, and I'm sure this birthday is no exception. She holds out a box tied with a silver ribbon. Asha picks at the tape carefully, trying not to tear the hand-stamped, personalized wrapping paper, but Emma finally exclaims, "Go ahead. I know you want to tear it."

Asha gives a happy sigh and rips the paper to shreds with great satisfaction. Inside the box is a knitted hat in a dark plummy purple—Asha's favorite color. She pulls it out, and she and I ooh and ahh over it.

"I made it," Emma says proudly. She taught herself to knit last month. "See that ribbon woven in across the center?"

Asha and I both nod.

"It's from the yellow ribbon we got for participating in the science fair in eighth grade. Remember?"

Of course we remember. Asha pulls the hat on over her dark hair and grins. "I'll wear it tomorrow on the slopes," she promises.

And I'm sure we'll see a selfie. #IAmAshaMirza wearing a hat.

"And here's something for fun." Emma grins, then hands Asha a small pink shopping bag. Emma always likes to add in a silly gift, too. That somehow makes her even more perfect.

Asha raises her eyebrows, reaches inside the bag, and digs around in the tissue paper like a squirrel searching for a nut.

I can't stand the suspense. "What is it?"

Asha pulls something out of the bag. It is a red baby-doll nightie with tiny little spaghetti straps and lots of lace.

"OMG." Asha bursts out laughing. She's the kind of girl who wears a huge T-shirt and sweats to bed. There is nothing more opposite to Asha's style than this nightie. And that's why it's so funny. Honestly, it's not something any of us would wear. It seems like a cliché from a movie.

Emma giggles. "Remember when we saw this at the mall? I thought you'd maybe want to take a picture and show it to Nate."

"Like, as a joke?" Asha rolls her eyes. "I'm not putting it on." She turns to Emma. "You do it."

"I'm not doing it," Emma says between giggles.

"It's my birthday, so I get what I want," Asha says, pushing the lace toward Emma. "And I want *you* to put it on."

I'm still laughing, but then I see Asha's face and I know she's serious. Emma sees it, too, and suddenly, nothing about this is funny.

Emma folds her arms over her chest, chin stuck out defiantly. She gets to her feet, towering over Asha. "You can't make me."

Asha's eyes narrow and she gets to her feet, too. "Looks like the space cadet woke up all of a sudden and got a backbone."

My stomach squeezes. Suddenly, we're back in middle school. Emma on one side and Asha on the other. Now Asha's birthday will dissolve into a fight.

Don't say anything. Let them settle this.

But I can't. My role as peacemaker has been years in the making. I step in between the two of them—arms stretched wide to keep them apart—and do the stupidest thing possible.

"I'll put it on," I say frantically. I take the scrap of red material from Asha's fist and hold it against my body so they can see the ridiculousness of the idea.

Suddenly, they are both laughing. Evidently, the only thing more comical than Asha wearing this outfit is the idea of me trying it on.

"Yes, try it!" Emma says. "Better Skye than me."

If I looked like you, Emma, I wouldn't care about wearing this stupid thing.

"I was kidding," I say. "Look. There's no way this will fit me." I shake my head vehemently, but instantly see the disappointment in their eyes. I will let them down and ruin the whole mood. But I have the power to fix it. I just have to make a fool out of myself for their entertainment.

Anything to keep the peace.

As usual.

"Come on, Skye," Asha wheedles.

And I give in. Like I always do. "Okay. Okay. Okay." I take the tiny scrap of lace and head toward the bathroom. "Wait a second."

"I'll put on the right music," Emma calls out as I slip into the bathroom and close the door behind me.

What have I agreed to now?

I change quickly out of my jeans and T-shirt. Then I'm struck with the realization of just how small this thing really is. I tug the scratchy lace down over my chest. Fatty rolls of skin bulge up over the V-necked front and under my arms. It's so tight around my stomach I can hardly breathe. The short lace hem only reaches to the tops of my fleshy thighs. I tug at the hem, uncomfortable even without an audience, but the material refuses to budge.

Everything about this is a huge mistake. But I remind myself it's just Emma and Asha outside that door. Now that I've gone this far, I might as well go all the way. I remove my ponytail, lean over, and toss my hair into a wavy mess with my hands. When I flip back up, the reflection in the mirror is a bit scary—lots of bare skin and big hair—but I figure it will definitely do the trick and get major laughs from both of them.

I throw open the door and step out to the opening chords of Lady Gaga's "Born This Way." The music is blaring and I stride across the room in an exaggerated cat-walk strut. The straps slip down off my bare shoulders, but I don't care. My goal has been realized. I have saved the day. Asha and Emma are laughing so hard they can barely talk.

"Work it, girl," Emma calls out.

And I do. I glance over one shoulder, tossing my hair back from my face in fake slow motion. Bending forward, I kiss the air in my best supermodel imitation.

Asha whistles and Emma is making loud whooping noises.

It is just us and I have to admit, I love making them laugh. I ramp it up even more, prancing and twirling across the room.

"Skye. Skye," Asha calls out. "Look this way."

I twist around to blow another kiss in her direction, but then catch my reflection in the sliding glass door. Everything stops. I freeze midspin, yanking up the straps on the nightgown. I don't know who that girl is with all the red lace, curves, and skin—but it isn't me.

"Oh. My. God," Asha squeals. "Don't quit now! That's perfect."

I look from my reflection to Asha. Her phone is out in her hand. She's filming me.

No. No. No.

I panic, holding out my hands to block the camera. There were only supposed to be two people watching me prance around in practically nothing, but Asha just let the world in.

"Stop, Asha. Erase it," I beg her, grabbing for the phone.

She holds the phone out of my reach. "It was live on ChitChat. I can't erase it yet, but relax. I'll delete it in fifteen minutes. Promise."

I feel horror clutch at me. "Asha! Hundreds . . . thousands . . . of people can see it by then!" I sputter.

Asha rolls her eyes at my reaction. "Only if they're on ChitChat, like, now."

Fifteen minutes feels like a lifetime.

"Don't freak out," Asha says. There is a sudden tone in her voice, and a sharp flash in her eyes—almost too quick to catch, but I see it. She thinks I'm overreacting and silly. If we were ten years old again, she'd call me a baby and make me cry.

Emma is studying the video on her phone, via ChitChat. "You look great. Want to watch it?"

I shake my head frantically, determined not to cry. "No, I want it to go away."

"And it will," Emma says soothingly. "Just give it a few minutes, then, *poof* . . . your time as a supermodel is history."

"I'm sorry. It's just that I'm . . . ." My voice dwindles off into silence.

"Crazy?" Asha asks. That edge is still in her voice.

"I was going to say super sensitive," Emma says, patting me on the shoulder.

Asha rolls her eyes. "I don't know why you have to be so self-conscious, Skye."

Live in my skin for sixteen years. Maybe you'll get it.

I take a deep breath. "Let me see it."

"Are you sure?" Emma asks.

I nod, but I'm not sure at all.

Emma holds out her phone and I look down at the screen. The video starts with a pan of the room, then focuses in on the closed bathroom door. Suddenly, the door opens, and a girl stalks out in a red nightie. *Oh. My. God.* The back of my neck is on fire, the flames rushing up into my face.

That girl in the video is me.

I can't stop watching. My skin is white and flabby, rolling over the tight strips of red in all the wrong places. But my face is so proud. So stupidly happy. Like I don't even know how horrible I look.

Make it stop. In a panic, I push frantically at the screen.

"See. You look fine." I hear Asha's voice like it's far away. "I told you. It isn't that bad."

People—*everyone*—will watch this video and think I want to be seen this way. I look up from the screen, eyes wide.

"Emma, take it down," I beg.

She shrugs sympathetically. "You know I can't."

"Oh, good grief," Asha says, grabbing Emma's phone from me. "Just change back into your clothes, Skye. If it'll make you feel better, I'll try on that stupid thing now. But no ChitChats!"

A few minutes later, with Emma and me sitting on the couch in our pajamas, Asha walks out for her big reveal. It doesn't make me feel better. In fact, it makes me feel worse. A lot worse. Asha looks perfect in anything, even in the ridiculous red nightie. Slim waist. Strong legs. With her long black hair and fierce attitude, she could be a Victoria's Secret model. And, even though she looks fantastic, no one dares take a video or a photo without her permission.

I'm the only stupid cow in the room.

Emma looks out the window and lets out an excited yelp.

"It's snowing!" she cries.

She points toward the sliding glass doors. I glance out at the beauty of the thick flakes suddenly swirling around.

"Let's go outside!" Asha declares. Even though she's still in the red nightie, she throws on her coat, yanks on her new hat from Emma, and steps into boots. Emma follows suit, putting her jacket and scarf on over her pj's. In a second, they are both out the sliding glass doors, leaving me sitting alone on the couch.

The cold air pours in through the open doors, cooling my flushed cheeks and bringing goose bumps to my arms. I blink hard, willing the tears not to fall.

"Come on, Skye!" Emma yells back inside, gesturing wildly for me to join them.

Asha calls out, "Just put on a coat." She is leaning over the edge of the deck, filming the snowflakes landing on Emma's hair. But all I can think about is that other video still floating around out there in the world for—I look at my watch—seven more minutes.

I take a deep breath, then pick up my coat and put it on, buttoning it all the way up to my neck, covering every inch of skin. I slip my bare feet into my boots and stumble across to the doorway. Emma grabs my hand, pulling me out onto the deck.

The lights from the houses on the lake throw out an eerie white glow onto the water as the snow slowly starts to cover the icy perimeter. Asha catches snowflakes on her tongue. Emma scoops up a handful of snow from the balcony railing and opens her fingers up to let the soft whispers of white blow off into the wind. It's one of those moments you know you should remember.

Asha grabs Emma and they twirl around in the cold

holding hands, faces up to the clouds. "Isn't this the best?" Emma calls out to me.

"It's beautiful," I mumble, but I can't help checking the time again. Three more minutes and then Asha can delete the video forever.

HARMONY

The wind is cold when she steps off the bus into the dark. Harmony Heaven sticks her hands down deep into the pockets of her black wool peacoat and feels the torn lining inside.

The Old Town stop is deserted, but within a block there are couples and families out for dinner under thousands of tiny white holiday lights. She walks past trendy boutiques, college bars, and restaurants where one meal would cost her a week of her Kmart salary. Maybe more. She isn't sure because she's never been inside any of those places. One time she did stop long enough to read the items on the menu. Then she checked in online like she'd actually been there. Later, she Googled the eighteen-dollar pasta Bolognese and found out it was just fancy spaghetti with meat sauce and not worth the three hours it would take standing at a Kmart cash register to pay for it.

Tucking herself into the doorway of the Linden Street Café, Harmony retrieves her pay-as-you-go phone out of her coat pocket. She logs on to the spotty free public Wi-Fi and sinks down onto the cold sidewalk. She pulls her coat closer around her body and leans forward into the welcome glow of the screen.

A trio of laughing college girls in high heels stumble by, but they don't notice Harmony huddled there in the dark or, if they do, they quickly look away. She's used to it. The internet is what gives her a connection to other humans anyway.

Harmony clicks through the open windows of other people's lives. Skye has posted a picture of herself with her two besties eating chocolate birthday cake. *Birthday parties*. Harmony can't remember the last time she saw a birthday cake, much less one with her name on it. She recognizes Skye's friends from school and the couple of times when they came in to heckle Skye at the service desk. The dark-haired friend is named Asha. The gorgeous blonde is named Emma. Harmony studies their faces. Pretty, happy girls. For a moment, Harmony lets herself imagine how her life might have been different if she had been born into Skye's world. It all seems so random.

Harmony decides to follow both Asha and Emma on ChitChat. When she opens Asha's profile, she sees a ChitChat video of Skye prancing across the room in a red nightie.

Interesting. Definitely didn't see that one coming.

And that is exactly why ChitChat is so addictive. You never know what you'll see. Harmony watches the video again. She hates that she's feeling lonely and more than a little jealous. Skye is there, joking and laughing it up in front of adoring friends. And Harmony is here.

Harmony glances up from the screen, distracted by the cold. She wishes she could stay online longer, but the snow is falling harder now and her fingers are tingling. Cellular minutes are precious when you pay as you go.

Reluctantly, she logs off and pulls herself up the wall with a groan. She slides the phone into her backpack, next to her only other prized possession—a battered paperback copy of *Anne of Green Gables*. Harmony carries it around with her everywhere because she never knows when there might be a chance to steal away to Prince Edward Island. She found the book in a giveaway box at the library and read it three times. Then she found the subsequent books and read the whole series while sitting in the worn chairs of the downtown library.

Now Harmony softly traces a finger across the cover. Anne is wearing a big straw hat, surrounded by flowers and fields, and she is walking home to Marilla and Matthew.

In another world.

Harmony steps out of the shelter of the doorway and heads farther down the street, past Washington Park, recently walled off with construction fences to make way for newer, fancier restaurants.

Slipping in the back door of Old Town Athletic Center, she nods at Billy, the night manager who lets her come in and work out in exchange for cleaning the locker rooms and mopping the bathroom floors. He even gives her some lessons if the night is particularly slow.

In the corner of the empty gym, she finds the punching bag. She changes her shoes and laces up her gloves and soon she's slugging and kicking the bag until her muscles scream. She throws a right cross and follows with a hard front kick. For these few minutes, she feels totally in control. When she's done, she pulls out her phone and takes a picture of the gloves on the gym floor. She wants to be a part of something bigger and she needs this contact. She wants someone out in there to know that she at least has *this*.

Harmony checks in at "Old Town Gym," posts the photo, and then captions it with the hashtag: #superpower.

Then she scrolls through ChitChat some more, wondering what Skye and her friends are up to now.

EMMA

Saturday afternoon, back at home, Emma blinks away the lingering exhaustion from last night's slumber party. She just got back from the Lyric Cinema's information session for their contest, and she needs to get inspired.

She sits down on her bed, puts in her earbuds, and pulls up YouTube on her iPad to watch a clip from her favorite movie, *Breakfast at Tiffany's*. All the voices outside her bedroom door mute.

On the small screen, it is pouring rain and Holly Golightly is searching for Cat. Of course, Emma would rather see the film in the theater. That's why she spends so much time in the darkened Lyric Cinema. Weeknights are her favorites. It is usually slow, especially for the foreign films with subtitles. Sometimes, she is the only one in the audience. Nothing beats that.

But at least watching here on her iPad, she has the control to watch her way. Emma slows down the scene at the end, concentrating on every frame. Then she rewinds and watches it over. And over again.

The information session was great. The head judge, Alexander, who runs the Lyric Cinema, explained all the rules. Anyone participating has to write a screenplay for a short film inspired by an old classic. First they have to submit their concept and get it approved. Then they have to write the screenplay and send it to the judges. The first prize is a summer trip to New York City for a film class in SoHo.

Everyone thinks Emma loves movies because she wants to be an actress, but she doesn't care about being in front of the camera. She wants to be a screenwriter. A director. A producer. Ideally, all three.

She dreams of mapping out scenes, directing every detail to wring out every emotion possible from actors. Emma is determined to make the story happen, not let it happen to her. She wants to call the shots. She wants to make the actors move a certain way. She wants to look at the situation from a different angle. She wants to make everything happen.

But most of all, Emma wants to go to New York City. Just like Holly Golightly in *Breakfast at Tiffany's*, she considers herself a wild thing. Eventually she'll get strong enough to run into the woods or fly over to a tree. And then to a higher tree. And then to New York City. This contest is only the beginning.

Emma hears more arguing outside her door. *Breakfast at Tiffany's* isn't doing enough to drown out the noise of her family. She closes out of the clip and searches for a different old movie to inspire her.

CHAPTER THREE

SKYE

My dog, Cassidy, greets me at the door with excited barks and wild tail wagging. This greeting is the same whether I'm gone for an hour or a day. Her unconditional joy is comforting, especially since I feel like I just got run over by an eighteen-wheeler. I kneel to hug Cassidy tight for a few seconds, her soft brown fur against my face, before letting her bound away.

Mom is sitting at the dining room table, her laptop open in front of her. Mom's a bookkeeper—I got my math smarts from her—and sometimes has to work weekends.

She looks over the top of her computer to greet me. "Hey, how was the party?"

"Okay," I say. "I'm tired."

"Did you get any sleep last night?" My mom closes the computer screen partway to give me her attention. She's wearing a black hoodie over her workout gear, but I doubt she actually went to the gym.

"Not much." I sit down in a chair beside her, my fingers drumming restlessly on the tabletop.

After we ran around outside in the snow, Asha, Emma, and I watched a movie of Asha's choosing and then went to bed. The two of them fell asleep right away, but I was up most of the night, tossing and turning and thinking about the ChitChat video. It had long since disappeared from the app, but it was still playing in my mind.

Cassidy joins us, her head finding my lap for a snuggle and ear strokes.

"What time are you working today?" Mom asks.

"Afternoon shift. Then I'm going over to Luke's afterward."

She nods. "Want something to eat?"

"Grilled cheese?" I ask hopefully. "And tomato soup with stars?"

Even though we both know I can prepare this meal myself, Mom laughs and gets up to go to the fridge. "Boy, you must be in a mood."

She knows me so well. I sigh. Moms and comfort food are the best when you're really tired and cranky.

A few minutes later, Mom's back with the sandwich and hot soup. I take a big bite, blissfully chewing, and Mom sits back down across from me. She tilts her head to one side and her eyes get serious. "By the way, is Asha's mom sick?"

"I don't think so. Why?"

"I was talking to Mrs. White down at the cul-de-sac yesterday."

Mrs. White is the neighborhood gossip. She has long gray hair and sort of resembles her shih tzu, Mitzie.

My mom continues the story. "Mrs. White works with Asha's mom at the university and said she's been out on some kind of extended sick leave. Did you see Asha's parents last night or this morning?"

I think about it, then shake my head. Asha, Emma, and I were ensconced in Asha's private section of the house the whole time.

"No, but I'm sure she's fine," I reply, chewing my sandwich. "Asha would have told me if something was wrong." *Just look at her posts and you'll see everything's perfect.*

My younger sister, Megan, and her best friend, Lulu, rush into the room like there's a serious emergency. "Oh good, you're home," Megan says to me. "Can you dye my hair?"

I look over at Mom and she shrugs.

"Why? Your hair is pretty the way it is," I say, reaching out to tug on Megan's shoulder-length ponytail.

"No offense, Skye," Lulu says in her pretentious, too-old-for-middle-school tone. Lulu has a smooth blonde bob that she swishes importantly across the tops of her shoulders for emphasis. "But that brown is kind of . . . you know . . . bland."

"Offense taken," I grumble, then blow on my spoonful of soup. Megan is a mini-me—same brown hair, same hazel eyes, same round face, same curvy figure.

"My hair needs to be bright red," Megan says. "I'll figure out the green skin later."

I stop with my spoon halfway to my mouth. "Seriously?"

"We're cosplaying. I'm going to be Gamora." Megan eyes the second half of my sandwich. "Are you going to finish that?"

"Yes," I say, and take a big bite right out of the middle of the piece just to prove it. She scowls at me.

"Who is Gamora?" Mom asks, obviously confused by the whole conversation.

"*Guardians of the Galaxy*?" Lulu rolls her baby-blue eyes and swishes her hair over one shoulder again. "Duh."

I think Lulu needs to read up on likability, too. "Hair dye is a little too drastic," I tell Megan. "I'm sure we can find a wig online that will be even more realistic. Besides, you never know who you'll want to be next week."

Megan thinks this over. "That could work," she says at last.

I pull off a corner of my sandwich—the crunchy, toasty edge Megan likes the most—and hand it to her. She grins, takes a bite, and leads Lulu back upstairs.

Luke's cheeks are flushed from the heat of the kitchen. His golden hair is damp from his baking efforts, making his curls a tousled mop. He bites his lip in concentration as he closes the oven door, peering inside with deep concern.

When he finally turns back to me, he pushes his hair out of his eyes with a big purple oven mitt and flashes me a grin.

"Almost ready."

I smile back. A red apron covers his T-shirt and he smells like vanilla and sugar.

"It smells delicious," I say from where I sit at the kitchen table.

I have my homework stacked in front of me but I can't focus. I'm still thinking about that stupid video Asha took. I need to concentrate on this assignment; otherwise my A in physics could slip away.

"Did you know the internet was originally called the Galactic Network?" I ask Luke, looking up from my book.

"Is that on your physics test?" Luke asks, confused.

"No. I just read it online somewhere." I close the book, giving up on studying for now. "And they called the people who first used it Internauts."

Luke shakes his head in amazement. He doesn't really understand my fascination with random facts. "You are an expert on everything."

"No, I'm an *Internaut*."

"Cool, Internaut Skye." He gives a gesture that is sort of a combination Vulcan and Boy Scout salute. "Be careful out there on that Galactic Network. Just don't go where no one's gone before . . ."

Suddenly, I have a horrible thought. "Were you on ChitChat last night?" I ask Luke.

"Nope," he says. "I was coming home from the soccer game. Remember? We won?"

I grimace. That was an important game. I should remember these things. "Oh yeah. Sorry."

At least I know he didn't see the video.

"So big plans for your day off tomorrow, huh?" Luke says, leaning over the counter. His eyes are almost the exact color of his faded green Abercrombie T-shirt. "Around two o'clock?"

I'm surprised. It's not like Luke keeps close tabs on me. He's never been a clingy boyfriend.

"Yeah. Asha, Emma, and I are getting mani-pedis then. How did you know?"

"I used the Galactic Network." He winks at me. "Emma posted about it earlier after she made some obscure movie quote references."

If only I could spend all my spare time watching movies like Emma. "Audrey Hepburn?"

"I think so."

I wonder how the information session at the Lyric Cinema went for Emma. Asha, of course, has been posting nonstop updates from her day snowboarding with Nate.

I glance down at my phone, instinctively checking my email. No new messages. I guess it was silly to expect to hear from Senator Watson's office on a Saturday. Although rumor has it her staff works around the clock.

Like he can read my mind, Luke asks, "Any news from the senator's office?"

I lean back against the chair and unfasten the clip from my hair. I run my fingers through my waves and redo the ponytail while he waits for my answer. "No," I finally say.

"You're going to get an interview," Luke says. "You have your 'to-do list,' right?" He laughs, making quote marks with his fingers.

"I do." I give him a big, extra fake smile.

"Do you take suggestions from the audience?" he asks. "For what to put on the list?"

"What do you want to add?"

"Go to all of Luke's soccer games."

I laugh. "I don't think that's going to help my political career."

"It can't hurt." He leans over further, giving me a quick kiss on the lips for emphasis. "Look, you've already come this far in student council," he points out.

"I guess," I say, and there's a moment of awkwardness between us.

Sophomore year, I lost the runoff election for student council vice president. This year I won. And I can't deny that it has to do with the fact that this year, I'm Luke's girlfriend. People may say politics isn't about popularity. But it is.

I know it is.

"The thing is," I say, brushing off the feeling of discomfort, "I want to do more than decide what snacks to have in the vending machines."

"Barbecue potato chips," Luke says.

I let out a frustrated sigh. Sometimes I feel like Luke doesn't get me, but I don't say anything. After all, Luke is the cute, super popular boy and I'm the girl no one imagined him ever dating.

"Just kidding." He gives me that smile that makes all the freshmen girls follow him around like lovesick puppies. "You *did* set up the whole job fair. That's impressive."

"Thanks," I say, feeling a warm glow. Organizing the school job fair has taken up a lot of my time for the past two months. "But how embarrassing will it be if I don't have an interview there?"

"Well, even if you don't get an interview with Senator Watson, there are plenty of other possibilities."

My smile disappears from my face. *Here we go again.* "Luke, come on. This is a big deal for me."

He shrugs. "I'm just saying it wouldn't hurt to check out all your options. I know how you are about this stuff. If you get that internship, it will suck up all your time."

"This *stuff* is important," I say fiercely. "Only sixteen-point-four percent of US Congress members are women. And Senator Watson wants to support young women in leadership. Like me."

"I know. I know," Luke says. "This is your big chance, but it's just not your *only* chance. My dad still has that receptionist position open and he'd be flexible with the hours."

Luke is trying so hard and I'm telling him things he already knows, but I can't stop myself. "Senator Watson is thirty-one years old and the youngest representative ever elected from Colorado. She has one internship position open for the summer." I hold up my index finger for emphasis. "One."

"But if this doesn't happen, there are other ways to spend the summer . . ." His voice trails off when he sees the expression on my face.

"You don't believe I can make it." I didn't know that was going to come out of my mouth, but there it is.

"That isn't true." He looks down at the counter, then back up at me. "I'm just saying things don't always happen the way you plan. But it doesn't mean it's *not* going to happen."

I don't need this. Not from him. A fast, raw anger runs up my neck and into my cheeks. Luke is supposed to be on my side no matter what.

"Forget it," I say in a tone that says I'm definitely not going to.

He starts to say something, but then stops himself and turns back to the stove, his shoulders slumping in resignation. The anger seeps out of me. I love those shoulders. I've seen them bare and sunburned in July after a long day on the lake. I've felt them covered by a fleece jacket and smelling of campfire in October, when we huddled together over steaming-hot cups of cocoa on a camping trip in the mountains.

Instantly, I feel guilty. "I'm sorry," I tell him. "I didn't get much sleep last night at Asha's, but I shouldn't take it out on you."

Luke shrugs but doesn't answer. Instead, he puts the other oven mitt on his hand and carefully opens the oven door.

When his father walks into the kitchen, I'm thrilled for the interruption of our awkward silence.

"Hi, Mr. Barrett," I say, shifting in my chair.

"What's up, Skye? Good day at the office?" He chuckles and I smile at him. He always makes lame jokes about my job, but I know he doesn't mean it in a bad way. It's more like he doesn't have anything else to talk to me about, so it's either school, work, or the weather.

"No problems today, Mr. B." I always feel a little uncomfortable around Luke's parents. Maybe because there are two of them—a mom and a dad—but also because they always seem so happy all the time. It's not what I'm used to.

"What about that mean girl?" Mr. Barrett loves my stories about all my coworkers.

"Harmony works the late shift tonight, so I didn't see her today."

"And that's why you didn't have any problems," he says, nodding with satisfaction.

"What's that smell?" Luke's mom comes through the back door. "New creation?"

"I'm working my way through a new cookbook of French desserts." Luke puts one finger on his lips and carefully closes the oven door. "Tonight, we shall have cappuccino soufflés."

"You never fail to amaze me." Mrs. Barrett smiles and pulls Luke in for a quick hug. I feel the familiar pang. It's something like jealousy, regret, sadness—all rolled together into a ball in my stomach that Luke's family kicks around sometimes. They should have a sitcom on the Hallmark Channel.

"Are you guys going out somewhere later?" Mr. Barrett asks.

"Maybe a movie," Luke says. He looks over at me and I shrug.

"You need some money?" And just like that, Mr. Barrett pulls out his wallet and gives Luke a couple of twenties.

I look down at my textbook, flipping pages randomly. My mom told me and my sister over and over again that we weren't the reason my parents got divorced. If it wasn't about us, and I'm honestly not so sure about that, then it must have been about money. They argued about it all the time, especially once Dad moved out. But then money got all mixed up with me and my sister, so it was hard to tell the difference. My mom was always on the phone telling my dad how much it cost to feed us, to buy us clothes. My mom still makes comments to her friends or family from time to time about my dad's lack of child support payments. It sort of makes me feel like some unwanted stray begging for scraps. I don't think she knows I hear.

But I do.

Mr. and Mrs. Barrett leave the kitchen, and Luke turns back to the oven to navigate the removal of the soufflés. My phone buzzes in my pocket. I pull it out. Weird. It's a text without a name or number attached. How can someone do that? Is that even possible?

The message says, **I HAVE SOMETHING FOR YOU, SKYE, AND YOU'RE NOT GOING TO WANT TO MISS IT.**

I'm confused. Normally, I would just delete something like this. But the sender knows my name. It's not some random spam. Still, it doesn't look like any text I've ever seen before. Maybe it's the interview committee, although it seems like a really strange way to contact me. Another text pops up on my screen.

THIS IS A TEST. NOT HARD. ARE YOU READY?

A test? Now my nerves are starting to kick in. I write back.

ME: WHO IS THIS? WHAT ARE YOU TALKING ABOUT?

The message comes back immediately. **CHECK OUT MY ACCOUNT ON CHITCHAT—@TELLTALE♥**

I glance at Luke. He's busily dusting powdered sugar over the top of his creations, a satisfied smile on his face.

I click on the link. It takes me to a blank ChitChat page. There is no profile photo or bio. No posts. Nothing but a pale pink background just sitting there like it's waiting for something.

Strange.

"Hello?"

I look up to see Luke standing in front of me.

"I just got this weird text about a ChitChat profile . . ." My voice trails off as I look back down at my phone.

Luke gives a frustrated sigh. "Is that phone more interesting than me?"

I don't answer. Then a new text, from the same anonymous number, comes in, along with photo.

LOOK AT THE PICTURE.

I do. And at first I don't even recognize myself. Everything about this is wrong.

It's a screenshot. Of me. From the video at Asha's

birthday party—only one frame frozen onto the tiny screen of my phone.

The image was obviously chosen for maximum shock value—picked at the exact moment that puts me in the worst possible light. It's a full-body shot—the nightie slipping down off one shoulder, and me leaning in to kiss the air with eyes half closed. My hair is big. My lips are pouty. But that's not the part of the picture I focus on. All I can see are my thick thighs, my round stomach, and my flabby arms. This is the me I've done everything in my life to hide.

Red heat crawls up my neck and into my cheeks. I am right there in all my size and skin, posing like I don't care what people think of me. And I do. I very much do.

I keep my face angled away from Luke, so he can't see my reaction and ask questions.

Who sent this to me?

Asha took the video, but she would never do something like this. She's the one who told me I had toilet paper stuck to my sneaker when I left the bathroom on Thursday, and to hold my skirt down tighter on that windy day last week. She would never embarrass me. When we were freshmen, Asha almost fought Michelle Speer when she said I looked like a circus clown in my red lipstick.

Emma isn't the fighting kind, but she gave Emory Mysik the silent treatment for almost a year for telling people about my dad leaving. It couldn't be either of my besties.

But they were the ones who were there.

"Is it about the interview?" Luke asks me.

Instantly, I'm reminded of everything I have to lose. I've been to three assemblies at school this year about preparing for college and the future. Every speaker mentioned the internet. Every. Single. Time.

Keep your online image clean. Colleges look at these things. Employers look at these things.

"No," I say quickly. "It's just a stupid cat video someone sent me."

Now my heart is starting to pound even harder. Senator Watson is not going to hire me with this kind of stuff floating around the internet. She is all about strong, powerful women and positive images. I can't let this photo go anywhere beyond my phone screen right now.

"The soufflés are ready," Luke announces, his face proud over the plate he's now holding out toward me. He is smiling this half smile that I know oh so well. His eyes are calm and soft. Completely trusting.

For a second, I think about showing him the screenshot. Telling him everything. But no. I tug on the hem of my denim button-down shirt, wanting to be sure my belly isn't exposed. If I show the photo to Luke, it makes it real.

That's not me. That's not who I am. Everyone knows that.

But that's not true. Senator Watson doesn't know that.
Or everyone at school. Or the people at work.

As Luke sets the plate of soufflés down on the table,
another text pops up on my screen.

**PAINT YOUR NAILS BLACK TOMORROW, OR
I'LL POST THE PHOTO ON MY CHITCHAT
ACCOUNT.**

How do they know I'm getting a manicure tomorrow? My
mind races back over my day. *Who did I tell?* I can't think.
This has to be Asha. I start to text her. Then I remember
Emma posted about our appointment online. Luke knew
about it. So it could be anyone . . .

I try to breathe. My head is reeling. *Please let this be a
joke. Please.*

Another new message comes in.

**FINGERNAILS AND TOENAILS. THEN POST
EVIDENCE ON CHITCHAT SO I'LL BE SURE YOU
DID IT. DO YOU UNDERSTAND?**

I don't know whether or not to reply. I *don't* understand. I'm being threatened? Why?

Luke reaches out and takes the phone gently out of my
hand. "Whatever it is can wait. The world's not going to
end if you don't look at that message right now."

"But . . . ," I say feebly. I lower my eyes as Luke puts the phone facedown on the table. It kind of feels like the world *might* end, but I don't say that.

My jaw is clamped down so tight I can feel the muscle in my cheek twitching. I put my hands on the table, pushing my palms flat against the surface to stop the trembling. If Luke asks me what's wrong, I'll blame the Venti Frappuccino I drank on my way over here. But Luke doesn't seem to notice my distress. He hands me a cappuccino soufflé with a big smile.

"Hope you love it," he tells me.

"It looks amazing," I mumble, but when I take a bite, I taste nothing.

ASHA

The air snaps with expectation and cold, but Asha rocks through it in typical breezy fashion. She pushes the volume up to drown out all thought and closes her eyes, letting the music in her earbuds slam into her brain. Her arms snake out in front of her in time to the rhythm and her Burton boots crunch through the soft powder beneath her feet. Even though she can feel the crust of the ice give under her, all she hears is classic Pearl Jam blasting, the song pounding down into her muscles.

It is a perfect day for snowboarding, and even though she finished the first two runs, it isn't over. Not by a long shot. A sculpted tunnel of white glitters in front of her like a billion tiny diamonds leading straight down the mountain. The pump of the adrenaline is still there from the last run, but now it is mingled with confidence. For Asha, snowboarding is about making the impossible possible in plain sight. It is about doing something wondrous and special, something that maybe humans aren't even meant to do. It is about leaving the mundane world of gravity behind.

Today it is also about forgetting.

She pushes that shadow out of her brain. Not now. Not here.

Another boarder steps out in front of her, smiling and holding out a gloved fist. Asha pulls out her earbud.

"You totally stomped that landing," Nate says with an admiring grin.

Asha bumps her own fist against his and grins back.

"You were great, too. Best run I've ever seen from you today," Asha says. She figures she might as well be gracious and share the love. The powder, the sun, and the clear blue sky make every boarder want the best run of the season. Asha balances her board against her side and unzips her baby-blue parka. "Besides, did you see me fall on that one jump? It was a total yard sale."

"Who cares, right?" Nate adjusts his helmet over his long blond dreads. "It's a gorgeous day for shredding the pow."

"It *is* pretty sweet," Asha admits, her smile growing until it takes over her face. After all, they are both after the same thing. Behind every cloud of breath and the ice-encrusted goggles are hopes of landing the seemingly impossible next trick.

"Photo op," Asha yells, and holds out her phone. Nate leans in, making a crazy face, and Asha snaps a picture of the two of them.

"Speaking of photos, are you gonna show me a pic of

the outfit you told me about? The one Emma got you?" Nate grins.

"Nope. You're not gonna get to see me in that thing just so you can show your friends or whatever." Asha sticks her tongue out at him and Nate laughs. Then she remembers the image she saved to her phone without telling Skye. "But you *should* see someone else in it!" she adds playfully, to get Nate off her case.

"Okay. I'll bite. Show me." Nate leans in to look at Asha's phone.

"Not so fast." Asha pulls it away. "You're going to have to work for it. You land that cab in the half-pipe and then we'll see."

Picking up his board and grinning back at her, Nate says, "See you at the bottom."

And now she is alone at the top of the run, the splendid snow tunnel in front of her, taunting her with its dazzling glory. This is Asha's happy place. She can't imagine wanting to be anywhere else on the planet. The Mirza family has been coming up to their condo in Steamboat for as long as Asha can remember. Her mother taught her to snowboard when she was only four.

Remember?

So many memories. They all come crashing in at once, like a continuous feed of photos.

Flash. Mom running alongside her while Asha rode a bike with pink and blue streamers blowing back from the handlebars. *Flash*. Asha and her mom jumping together on green chalk squares drawn on summer sidewalks. *Flash*. Blowing out candles on a birthday cake her mom made especially for her.

Remember?

Suddenly, standing on top of the world makes her feel totally alone. Like the inevitable is coming, but no one realizes it. It never used to feel that way. She shivers—an impulsive jerk that takes her by surprise. It isn't from the cold, or even from the anticipation of the steep drop-off in front of her. The shadows are back, and not even a perfect day on the slopes can keep them at bay. Switching her phone over to video mode, she films herself waving.

"Hi, Mom," she says to the camera. Then she posts it to ChitChat with her trusty hashtag: #IAmAshaMirza *boarding*.

Then she shoves the phone into her jacket pocket, zipping it up for safety. She pulls her goggles down over her eyes, blinking rapidly, then slides off downhill into a slow glide.

CHAPTER FOUR

SKYE

ME: WHERE R U GUYS?

Punctuality is part of my rule-following personality. Emma and Asha don't have that trait. It's Sunday afternoon, ten minutes past our appointment time. I'm waiting outside the nail salon on a bench facing a busy parking lot. I check the weird TellTaleHeart ChitChat profile one more time. Still nothing. No photos. No messages. No videos. It's just there waiting. Gathering followers.

Last night, I Googled around and figured out that the anonymous texts are coming from a free online service anyone can use. So that gave me no clues.

A text pops up on my screen now.

EMMA: ON MY WAY

Nothing from Asha. I click off my phone and slide it back into my purse. Then I stand and walk into the salon, over to the wall of nail colors. Pinks. Reds. Blues. Purple. Even green. Down at the bottom are the blacks.

I look at them all—except the blacks—picking up a few and examining them. Finally, I select a dark strawberry-pink color and shake it up to see it swirl around in my hand, like the thoughts whirling around in my brain.

I don't have to listen to whomever texted me last night. I should choose pink or purple like I always do.

But then I imagine that photo going everywhere.

Anger bubbles up from the fear. *This isn't funny.*

I pick a black bottle off the bottom shelf, curling my fingers tight around it to keep my hand from shaking. After a long minute, I pick up a pale pink, too, and carry both of them back to the pedicure station. I get in the first seat and Leah, the nail technician, twists some knobs. The water pours into the pedicure chair. I pull out my phone and type into my Notes app.

TO DO:
LEAD CONVERSATIONS WITH A COMPLIMENT
~~SMILE MORE~~

"I like your hair when you wear it curly," I tell Leah. My to-do list helps distract me from my worries. Plus, it feels good to look for something nice to say to someone.

Leah glances up, surprised, and fluffs her dark hair

around her shoulders. "Thank you. I didn't have time to do anything this morning, so I just let it dry naturally."

"You should do that more often," I say.

Leah puts a scoop of powdered soap into the water, and I tentatively dip my toes in. It's scalding. I glance over at the black nail polish perched on the arm of my chair.

If Asha is the one who sent me the texts, I *could* call her bluff. But then, I know Asha. She never bluffs.

It has to be her. Asha's always doing things like this to other people—posting unflattering photos or making snarky comments. Now it's my turn to be her victim.

And it's not like she's never done this kind of stuff to me before.

Suddenly, I remember when Asha gave me, the fattest kid in seventh grade, a gigantic Hershey's Bar at my birthday party. Everybody laughed because it was funny, right? It has to be what every fat girl wants for her twelfth birthday. And it's even funnier when you give it to her in front of the whole class, wrapped up in gold shiny paper.

Then there was the time, when we were thirteen, when Asha made me ride the Ferris wheel at the state fair even though I said I'd throw up.

I did.

And the other time, when we were fourteen, when she insisted I ski the double black diamond trail even though I said I wasn't ready.

I wasn't. And I almost broke my leg.

The memory of these betrayals makes my back stiffen against the chair.

"Sorry we're late!"

Asha rushes into the salon with Emma trailing behind her.

I roll my eyes at them, but they pick out colors quickly and come back to the chairs beside me in record time.

"Is the water okay?" Leah asks me.

I nod. It's cooled off now.

Asha and Emma settle into their seats, greeting the salon employees who will be doing their nails today. The three of us have been coming here forever.

I lean over Emma to talk to Asha, watching her reaction closely. "Your makeup looks perfect. You're going to have to give me some pointers," I say.

"Thanks," Asha says. She's not acting any different than normal.

What if it isn't Asha, though? Then what? Is it worse to think it's my best friend, or that it's someone else? Someone unknown?

Asha looks back down at her magazine and flips a few more pages.

Would Asha really be disloyal to me now? Would she threaten to damage my future just for a laugh?

The truth is, this TellTaleHeart person could be any-one who just happened to see the ChitChat video for those fifteen minutes on Friday night. *Anyone*. The thought makes my stomach hurt.

I bite my lip. Maybe the username—TellTaleHeart—is some kind of hint about who this person is and what they want. Is it a reference to "The Tell Tale Heart," that Edgar Allan Poe short story that was assigned to us in freshman year, about a murderer with a guilty conscious? Is the TellTaleHeart person hiding something, like the narrator of the Poe's story was hiding a body under the floorboards? I shudder.

"Did you pick your color?" Leah asks me.

I hand her the black polish with a little more force than necessary and look over to see if Asha has noticed. She's still flipping through the magazine, her whole body shaking with the motion of the massage chair. The headlines scrawled across the face of the gorgeous cover model read "Hollywood's Hottest Teen Star Gets Real" and "Selfie Skin—Camera-Ready Face, Eyes, & Hair." Asha doesn't look up, but that doesn't mean anything. I've seen Asha stare down Tom Ramirez, the biggest kid in ninth grade, just for stealing my homework. She didn't even flinch, and Tom finally gave my homework back with an apology.

Emma looks at the tiny black bottle I gave to Leah and frowns at me. "Whoa. Feeling a little Goth today?"

"I wanted something different."

Emma laughs. "Okay. Calm down. It's just nail polish."

An older lady getting fake nails applied turns and looks at us. My tone was way too defensive.

It actually isn't what I want at all, but if I do this stupid thing, the joke will be over.

"Relax, Skye," Leah tells me, pouring a long line of warm pink lotion down each of my legs. "You're so tense." She massages the lotion into my calves with deep circular motions, but it does not help my rising frustration.

"In China, royalty used to wear red and black nail polish," I say to my friends. I read that on the internet last night; I'd been searching for random facts about nail polish to make myself feel better.

"You are *not* Chinese royalty," Asha says.

I stick my chin out. "No, but I can wear whatever I want. It's a free country."

"So you're making nail polish a political statement?" Emma asks, confused.

No, it's about control.

Leah looks at me like I'm crazy.

Asha says to Leah, "Just ignore her. She's a walking compilation of weird historical facts."

"Whatever," I say.

I watch Leah uncap the bottle of black nail polish. She pulls the brush out of the bottle and then quickly coats my big toenail with the dark color. It makes my toes look like they are rotting off.

I hate it.

"Is this what you want?" Leah asks, looking up at me doubtfully.

I nod before I can change my mind, then sit in silence as Leah carefully paints each toenail black. The mold is spreading.

Emma is talking about the film competition at the Lyric. She has to write a screenplay inspired by a classic movie. The first prize is a trip to New York City for the summer.

Asha interrupts. "Nate and I were texting this morning and he said he was really into jazz," she says, surveying her newly sky-blue toenails.

"That's good, right? You like jazz," Emma says. I can tell she's a little annoyed that Asha interrupted her, but we both know it's better to let things slide.

"He misspelled it," Asha says.

"How do you misspell jazz?" Emma gives a snort of laughter.

"J-A-S-S," Asha says.

Nate is definitely not the brightest bulb in the socket.

"So he's out?" Emma asks.

"He was pretty cute on the slopes yesterday. But I think we're done."

I pull out my phone to take my mind off the color of my toes. I scan through different sites, looking into people's windows that are thrown open wide for strangers to see inside. For once, I think about someone looking back at me. It's not a good feeling.

Harmony is checking in again at random places. She is so strange. Who checks in at convenience stores? Then I see that Ryan has tagged Harmony in a photo, so it shows up on her wall. It's a cool picture—two faces reflected in the glass of an aquarium. The unusual angle makes it striking: almost like it's from the fish's point of view. I look closer and recognize the Kmart pet department. It's Dead Fish Man, and he's watching Harmony scoop out a new goldfish from the tank. He looks so happy and Harmony looks so determined. There is a story in that photo and it makes me want to see more of Ryan's photos. I click over to his profile.

He's tagged in lots of pictures—parties, friends, family. Just the regular stuff everybody posts. I wonder if that one girl who keeps tagging him is his girlfriend. Her name is Amy. With his quiet good looks, I'm not surprised he is so popular. I come upon a portrait of Amy that Ryan must have taken. Her face is heart-shaped and he has captured her midlaugh, with her head thrown back toward the sky. Just by looking at her photo, I can imagine the sound of her laughter. It would be contagious.

I keep scrolling. Ryan's a good photographer. I see more shots from Kmart, including a couple more of Harmony, some of Mr. King. All candids, taken from a distance. In one shot, I'm captured in the far background, standing at the service desk. I'm not tagged, thankfully. It's not the most flattering picture of me. I wonder if Ryan has taken any other pictures of me that I'm not aware of.

A sliver of an idea crawls into my brain. Maybe Ryan took the screenshot of me in red lace?

But why?

We finish up our pedicures and move to the manicure chairs. Asha is still talking about Nate, but all I can hear is *blah blah blah*. I try to calm the paranoia thrashing around inside my head, feeling my chest rise and fall with each breath.

"What shape do you want your nails?" Leah asks me, leaning over my trembling hands with a nail file at the ready.

As usual, Asha jumps in before I can answer.

"She likes her nails square. Just like mine."

A new idea occurs to me. *Did Asha share the video of me with Nate? Could* he *be the one threatening to share it?*

I can just imagine Nate looking at me in that tiny outfit stretched out over my bare skin.

My heart goes hard. The Galactic Network will work fast. Nate will share the screenshot with all the guys on the ski team. Then the ski team will share it with the cheerleaders. Then the upperclassmen will share it with the freshmen, and they will share it with the middle school. It doesn't matter that Nate lives four hours away. Someone will share it with someone I know.

That's how the internet works.

Teachers will eventually see it. Maybe even parents. The senator's office. My brain is spiraling down a deep, bottomless black hole. I feel my muscles tense up even more.

#IAmAshaMirza *stabbing you in the back*.

Finally, I can't take it anymore. Our hands and feet are tucked under the driers when I finally turn to Asha and ask, "Did you show anyone that video you took?"

"What video?" Asha asks.

"The one of me in the nightie. On your birthday. Did you show it to someone?" I repeat.

Emma looks up from her phone, and glances back and forth between Asha and me. She doesn't say anything. Maybe she already knows the answer.

Now I'm even doubting Emma? What is wrong with me?

"What do you mean?" Asha asks. "It was live, so yeah, I'm sure some people saw it." Asha shrugs like she doesn't even care. "But I deleted it. Remember? It's gone. No worries."

But it isn't gone.

When we're paying, I look down at my hands. It's like they have tiny chains wrapped around each finger, trapping me to the will of some anonymous someone out there.

As instructed, I take a picture of one hand and both feet, still in the salon paper flip-flops. The black polish is clearly visible. I post the photo to ChitChat. No caption, no hashtag. Let this TellTaleHeart person just see it so this whole thing can be over and done with.

An alert chimes on my phone and my heart sinks. Is there another text already?

No. It's an email. I'm afraid to open it. *What's the next challenge? Dancing naked on a street corner?* I finally look down at the screen.

"What's up with you?" Emma must have seen something in my face.

I look up to see both her and Asha staring at me. "It's an email from Senator Watson's office," I whisper.

"Read it, silly." Asha is pulling on my arm, but I step away so she can't read over my shoulder. If it's bad news, I don't want Asha seeing it.

What if it's a rejection?

Only one way to find out. I carefully click open the email. Emma and Asha wait. I can feel their stares.

I try to catch my breath as I read the email. "I have an interview at the job fair," I say. There is hope after all. I can barely believe it myself, but saying it out loud makes it real.

"Wait. With Senator Watson?" Emma asks excitedly.

"Well, not with *her*, but with her office. They're sending a representative to the school job fair!"

"Oh my God. That's amazing!" Asha grabs me and pulls me in for a tight hug. Pushing me away, she peers into my face. "You're excited, right?"

"Of course I am," I say in a daze of happiness. "This is what I've been working for and dreaming about."

"We have to celebrate!" Asha is pulling me side to side in a dance. Emma joins in and we all squeal and spin, while the whole nail salon looks on in confusion, a little cranky at the noisy interruption. Then Asha's phone is in her hand and, before I can stop her, she snaps a photo of Emma and me dancing and sends the news to everyone on the planet. I'm not even annoyed she's sharing it on social media before I have the chance to. I'm just too happy.

CONGRATS TO MY BFF, SKYE. SHE JUST GOT AN INTERVIEW WITH SENATOR WATSON'S OFFICE AT THE SCHOOL JOB FAIR! THIS GIRL WILL BE IN THE WHITE HOUSE ONE DAY!

I don't care about my stupid nails anymore. The strange text message was an obvious prank that had no real consequences. If that was all there was to it, and I certainly hope it was, then no real harm was done. The paint on my nails, the shimmer on my eyelids, the curl in my hair, the rings I wear. Mascara. Blush. Polish. Why does it matter? At the end of the day, you come home and wash it all off. The person who closes her eyes at night, scrubbed free of all the extra additions, is still the same person who wakes up to do it again the next morning.

The same person who will soon be headed to Senator Watson's office this summer and then, who knows?

On a break from the Kmart stockroom on Sunday, Ryan takes photos of Millie Johnson working in the paint department. He asks her permission and, while she may have thought it was a bit weird, she says yes.

"Make me look good," she says, and he promises he will.

Then he tells her one of his favorite quotes from photographer Dragan Tapshanov: "'Photography is about capturing souls, not smiles.'"

Millie smiles anyway, smoothing her gray curly hair back from her forehead and pushing her silver glasses up her nose. But it is definitely her kind soul that shimmers in her dark brown eyes.

Ryan can't bring his nice Nikon to work, so he uses the camera on his phone. The photos he likes best are not of Millie's face, but her hands. He loves the way her wrinkled, dark brown hands contrast with the blue, yellow, and green splotches of paint that speckle her skin. Last week he took pictures of puddles of water in the parking lot—shooting from a low level with his iPhone close to the water. And yesterday he took pictures of a well-loved teddy bear left behind on the linoleum floor, between rows of cold medicine and pain relievers.

The images are always there waiting for him. It isn't about what he sees, it's all about *how* he sees. He can't turn it off.

"Why are you always taking pictures in the store?" Skye asked him once when he was walking past the service desk.

"It's a hobby," he told her. But he didn't tell her he wants to take her picture. Not yet.

That night, Ryan sits at his kitchen table, uploading Millie's pictures onto his computer. He plays with edits and filters, trying to find the one image to upload to his web portfolio. The Squarespace website isn't public yet, but maybe someday he'll be brave enough to share.

"Who is that?" Ryan's mother leans over his shoulder to look at the photo on the screen. She is reheating the pork chops for him that the rest of the family ate for dinner hours ago while he was still at Kmart. There is a plate of lumpia on the table for him to eat while he waits.

"It's a woman at work. She works in the paint department." Ryan dips the crispy deep-fried rolls in sweet-and-sour sauce and takes a bite.

"Ha! Aren't there kids your age at work?" Mom asks,

putting the pork chops on the table while he pushes the computer out of the way. He knows his mom worries about his social life. She feels guilty for making him move so far away from his friends his senior year in high school.

"Sure there are," Ryan says, and he thinks about Skye. He thinks about how her long chestnut hair would look in a certain light and he thinks about how he'd like to capture the humor in those intelligent hazel eyes. There is something in her eyes that makes him want to know more.

Mrs. de la Cruz sits at the table while Ryan eats, asking more questions about his day. Every so often she comments in Tagalog to his dad, who sits over on the couch watching a basketball game.

His dad yells *"Susmariosep!"* at the television and his mother rolls her eyes. The game must not be going his way.

A constant bass pounding sound comes from upstairs. Ryan looks toward the ceiling, then over at his mother. "Is she still at it?"

His mom frowns, then nods. She seems pretty down lately about their move from California. Ryan knows she misses their big extended Filipino family and Sunday afternoons filled with games of mahjong with the aunties. But at least she has Lola here with her. Even if Lola spends most of her time in her room singing karaoke on her tiny portable player.

After dinner, Ryan goes upstairs. His room is down at the end of the hall, but before he makes it safely inside, he hears, "Pssst!"

His grandmother, a microphone in hand, stands at the door to her room. She is a head shorter than him, but it always feels like she is much bigger. "Tomorrow. *Yung ano . . .*"

"Yes," he says. "I haven't forgotten."

She nods in satisfaction, reaching up to give him a quick kiss on the cheek, then says, "Go change into your home clothes."

Later, Ryan sits on his bed, his computer in front of him. His cousin Amy is tagging him in photos again. She lives back in his old neighborhood in San Francisco. She's determined to give Ryan the best possible online cred to impress all the kids at his new school. Last Thanksgiving, she found out Ryan had never had an actual girlfriend. He'd gone on dates—to school dances and movies—and had even kissed a couple of girls. But there was never anyone special that he wanted to hang out with more than a few times. Ryan wishes he hadn't confided in Amy, but what's done is done. Now Amy is posting pictures and videos of all her friends, and tagging Ryan in each one. Amy's new mission, and crazy idea, is to make Ryan look super popular.

Amy and her friends dancing at a party in short skirts and high heels. *Tag.*

Amy's friends at the movies, with crazy dog filters on their faces. *Tag.*

Amy feeding fries to two of her girlfriends at In-N-
Out Burger. *Tag.*

Ryan leans back against the pillows and shakes his
head, the corners of his mouth tilting upward. Amy
means well, but she doesn't get it. He's not into photos
that try to make him look popular. He loves photography, but not these silly party shots and dog filters.

Ryan scans through some of his own photos that he
took back in California. Lately, he's been into portraits.
Amy and her friends were only too eager to pose. There
were a couple of good ones worthy enough to upload
to his portfolio. There's this one of Amy in silhouette in
front of the sunset, staring out at the Bay Bridge. Just
looking at it makes him homesick for foggy air and sea
smells, but that is the sign of a good photo. It makes you
feel something.

He scrolls through his ChitChat feed and stops on a
post from Skye. Her toenails, painted black.

Just for laughs, he opens her profile and studies
some of her older posts. He finds out new things he
never knew before. She has a big brown dog named
Cassidy and a younger sister named Megan. She'd
rather stream episodes of *The West Wing* than *Gossip
Girl*. There's her favorite music. There are things that
make her laugh. There's her favorite book—a slightly

battered copy of *Democracy in America*. One click leads to another and then to another, and he sees her life develop in front of his eyes. Each post brings Skye's personality into clearer and clearer focus.

Ryan has never watched *The West Wing* before. But he pulls up the first season on his computer and watches two episodes before drifting off to sleep with thoughts of Skye filling up his mind and spinning around in his head.

CHAPTER FIVE

SKYE

On Monday morning, the high school hallways smell like cafeteria Tater Tots and sound like a crowded freeway. Slower traffic grumbles along next to the lockers. The always rushed, always late plow through the center lane, yelling at everyone else to get out of their way.

I close my locker and push through the crowd, listening to the chatter around me. The end of the school year is sort of in sight, and a sense of relief and exhaustion is bubbling to the surface.

Being on the downward slide toward summer should be wonderful, but it seems like every conversation eventually turns to everyone's exciting, glamorous plans. *I've been accepted to do blah blah blah. I wonder who I'll meet when blah blah blah. I'm traveling abroad to blah blah blah.* Usually I'm terrified that I'm the biggest loser in this game of Future-ama.

But today feels different. I have hope. I have an interview with Senator Watson's office. Then I'll be able to join the conversations with news of my own. Not even my black-tipped fingers are able to ruin my mood.

Luke is against the wall by the trophy cases with his soccer team pals, saying hi to every single person who walks by. They all know him.

Luke couldn't care less about my nail polish. I give him a wave and a smile, but I don't go over there. He isn't one of those guys who thinks he has to drag a girl along by her hand everywhere to prove his undying love. That's not the kind of relationship Luke and I have. We don't have to be kissing in the middle of the hallway to be together. Besides, everyone knows we're a couple and they're totally over the shock of the überpopular jock guy with the curvy average girl. It's yesterday's news.

Until that screenshot makes it onto everybody's screens.

Any one of the hundreds of kids passing back and forth in front of me could be the proud owner of that stupid picture.

But which one?

Reese Jackson walks by holding hands with Edward Munoz. She's a math genius and he's a drum player in the jazz band. Reese paints her nails black a lot, but I don't know what she'd have against me. Then there's Marianne Washington, with her mouth full of braces and her two-kitties-hugging sweatshirt, alone by the door to the library. Marianne's by herself a lot. I feel a twinge of guilt. We were friends when we were in elementary school. I even spent the night at her house a couple of times. Then we drifted apart when I got close to Asha and Emma. Could Marianne be harboring some long-held grudge?

The bell rings and I head to class. In each period, I try to focus on what teachers are saying, but it's hard. Even though there've been no new messages from the TellTaleHeart person, I'm on edge. At first, I keep my hands in my pockets or tucked under a book. Then I realize that this mystery person might react in some way if he or she notices my nails. True, I posted a picture of my nails online. But if this person is a classmate, he or she might also be looking for evidence in real life.

If I can find some random acquaintance to pin this on, I tell myself, then I won't have to suspect my close friends.

And then I can ask that person the most important question of all.

Why me?

So I start putting my hands in front of everyone, trying to get a glimpse of some reaction. Kids talk to me in class, ask me about my weekend, sit at my table in my lunch, along with Luke and Emma and Asha. A couple of times over the course of the day, I almost open my mouth to ask some random passerby, "Are you the one?" But then I end up shutting my mouth again and swallowing down my questions.

Surprisingly, there is not one mention of my black fingernails by anyone.

So what was the point? This one small change didn't cause a ripple in anyone's opinion of me. Does my fingernail polish or what I wear cause anyone to like me more or less? *Of course not.* The anger in my chest lessens a bit. It was a stupid joke and now it's over.

On my way to English class, I'm surprised to see Ryan de la Cruz hanging out near my locker. Since he's a senior, we don't usually run into each other much at school. Work is our world.

"Hey," he says. "Can you remind the manager on duty that I'm going to be late tonight?"

"Sure. Anything wrong?" I open my locker door and glance over to see if he's looking at my hands. He's not.

Ryan shakes his head. "No. I just told my lola I would take her to look at some new apartments."

"Who's Lola?" I can't help but ask, putting in two books and taking out one. I wonder if he has a girlfriend.

"My grandmother."

"Oh," I say, feeling silly.

Ryan smiles. "Lola means *grandmother* in Tagalog. We're Filipino," he explains.

"Were you born in the Philippines?" I ask him. I realize I don't know too much about Ryan, and I'm a little curious now.

"Yeah, but my family moved to California when I was three. I've only been back to visit there a couple times."

"That's cool," I say. I've never left the state of Colorado, much less the country. I stash my copy of *Beowulf* for English into my bag. "So why does your grandmother want a new apartment?" I ask.

"She is living with us now, but she isn't happy. She says there's an old white woman ghost that hangs out in the hallway near the bathroom."

I laugh.

Ryan shrugs. "Ghosts aren't a laughing matter to my lola. That's why she wants new construction. No ghosts."

"Do your parents know about this?" I ask.

"They definitely know about the ghost. She tells them every time she has to go to the bathroom. Sometimes she even makes my mom stand outside the door," Ryan says, leaning against the wall beside the row of lockers. "But they don't know about her plans for a new apartment. She wants to keep it between us until she finds the perfect place. Then she's going to spring it on my mom."

I smile, enjoying this peek into Ryan's family. They sound nice.

"Good luck. Sounds like you're going to need it," I tell him.

"Thanks," he says.

I close my locker, leaving my hand—palm down, fingers spread—on the outside of the door a beat longer than usual. My black nails stand out against the light-blue metal like rust stains. It seems like Ryan *is* looking at my nails now. I frown at him. Suddenly, all the uncertainty rushes back.

As I turn to go, Marianne Washington wanders down the hall past us. She gives me a metallic grin. Quickly, I spin back to face my locker, blinking rapidly.

Is it her?

"Are you okay?" Ryan asks.

Or is it him?

I nod frantically. "I just need to get to class."

I slide into my desk a few minutes before class starts and watch the mad rush to beat the tardy bell. While I wait, I pick at the polish on my thumb. It chips off in a chunk, leaving my nail even uglier than before.

Asha makes it into the chair beside me with seconds to spare. Emma comes through the door as the late bell is actually ringing, so she has to sit in the front row. World Literature is the only class we all have together this semester.

From her desk at the front of the classroom, Mrs. Drager is asking about last night's assigned reading of *Beowulf.* Her voice trembles with excitement, like these 3,182 alliterative lines are the best things ever written. Mrs. Drager needs to get a life.

I can't concentrate. All I can think of is the screenshot. Even worse is the thought that someone I know may be threatening to share it. My black-tipped hands tremble. I wish I didn't care so much about looking stupid.

But I do.

I can't be exposed. That picture is everything I've tried to push down. If that photo leaks, nobody will see me beyond the image of a girl in a very tight, incredibly skimpy nightie. It will change people's opinions of me. Maybe I'm not as smart as they once thought. Maybe I'm fatter. Maybe I'm stupider. Maybe I'm shallower. Maybe I'm all of those things.

Voices of all the possible shattered expectations whisper through my brain.

Oh. My. God. Can you imagine her thinking she's all that?

Who put a fat, ugly cow in that nightgown?

What a loser!

I don't want to be an outside shell only—pudgy and pale. To know me, you have to peel back my skin and look inside.

"What are your first impressions of this epic poem?" Mrs. Drager asks, bringing me back to the classroom. She tucks a strand of streaked blonde hair behind her ear, then stands up purposefully.

Nobody says a word, but Mrs. Drager is stubborn about providing wait time. She leaves the question hanging out there for several uncomfortable beats of silence. She paces

back and forth in front of the desks like a warden surveying death row inmates.

I turn my head to look over at Asha. She's leaning forward over her desk, fingers dug into her long black hair,
frowning down at her open book like it contains Egyptian
hieroglyphics instead of Old English.

Could my best friend actually be blackmailing me? For fun?
The doubt makes me feel guilty, but I can't push it away.

It's time to try to say something again. I wasn't brave
enough in the nail salon.

I write a note in my notebook to Asha: *It's not funny.* I
put a big sad face in the margin and slide it over to her.

Asha looks puzzled. She writes back, *What?*

I'm wrong about her. I must be.

"Asha?" Mrs. Drager calls.

We're caught. I quickly cover up our notes with black
scribbles.

Asha has that deer-in-the-headlights look everyone gets
when they get called on in class and haven't finished the
reading assignment.

"Ummmm . . . there is a monster named Grendel."

"And?" Mrs. Drager freezes like she's spotted a rare
specimen in the wild and doesn't want to frighten it away.

I look down at my desk. So does everyone else. I pick
another chunk of black off my thumbnail and try to act
nonchalant. Cool. Like, *Yeah, I totally know everything
about* Beowulf.

"Skye?" Mrs. Drager asks. "Can you add to what Asha has said?"

My head shoots up. *Not really.* I slide my hands under my desk. "Beowulf cuts off the monster Grendel's arm and kills his mother."

Mrs. Drager says, "Beowulf actually *wrenches* Grendel's arm off. What does that mean?"

I wrinkle up my nose. "Beowulf pulled his arm off?"

There's a collective *ewwwww* from the class and Mrs. Drager sighs. She's clearly frustrated with our lack of enthusiasm for the discussion, but suddenly sees Emma's hand waving. Our teacher's face explodes with relief.

"Ms. Middleburg, I'm sure you can contribute something meaningful to this conversation. What can you tell us about *Beowulf*?" Mrs. Drager asks.

Emma brightens. "Did you know there is a 3-D movie of *Beowulf*?" she asks. "Angelina Jolie is the monster's mother."

Everyone perks up at the idea that they could watch the movie instead of read this complicated book, but Mrs. Drager doesn't seem impressed at all.

"There are actually quite a few differences between the movie *Beowulf* and the original poem," she says. "For example, in the poem, Grendel's mother is never described as being covered in gold. And she definitely doesn't look like Angelina Jolie."

The mood in the room bottoms out. I can almost hear the groans of disappointment. Evidently, watching the movie is not going to be a good substitute for the test. But then Mrs. Drager takes it even further.

"Emma, perhaps you can make a presentation to the class on the differences between the two next week."

Emma's face drops. Now she can't just watch the movie; she has to read the poem, too.

Touché, Mrs. Drager.

When the bell finally rings, Emma, Asha, and I leave the classroom together, like we always do. Emma is complaining about her new assignment and Asha is complaining about Nate. Suddenly, I feel silly about the note I wrote Asha. Maybe there's no reason to be so paranoid. Nothing has changed between me and my friends. I just need to rock my interview at the job fair, and then everything will be okay.

CHAPTER SIX

SKYE

Two days later, I sit behind the wheel of my parked blue Honda Civic, fingers tapping restlessly on the steering wheel. My shift at Kmart starts in five minutes and I will not go inside a second too soon.

I am using this valuable time to practice for my interview with Senator Watson's office. It's tomorrow. So I am sitting here alone, essentially talking to myself. I stare out the windshield in front of me as Kmart's automatic doors swish open and shut for customers coming and going.

"For me, this internship is all about learning," I say to the dashboard. "Interning with Senator Watson will give me the opportunity to work with a diverse group of people and help make our country better."

I say the last part all deep-voiced and dramatic, like I'm reciting a speech in front of hundreds. The silence in the car is not encouraging.

Even though I've tried to predict every possible question my interviewer might ask, my hands still get sweaty and my breathing gets faster each time I imagine the interview happening.

I know what will help me calm down. I take out my phone and update my to-do list.

TO DO:
MAKE EYE CONTACT
~~LEAD CONVERSATIONS WITH A COMPLIMENT~~
~~SMILE MORE~~

There. I feel better already.

I glance at the clock. My five minutes are almost up. No more delays. Soon, I'll have to enter the store and face that continual flow of needy strangers. They all come here because they want something. Or at least they think they do. Then they go on about their day at hospitals, and schools, and office buildings. And someone, somewhere out there, is happy at the end of the day when they return home and realize they remembered to buy toilet paper.

I get out of the car, reaching back inside for the hated blue smock lying across the passenger seat. It will be an agonizing transformation, buttoning it up over my T-shirt and jeans, but it's a necessary evil I can't avoid. I decide I'll put the smock on inside, where I can take off my coat. It's still cold out.

The weekend snow is mostly gone, leaving behind dirt-streaked mounds of ice in corners of the parking lot and muddy patches on the grassy medians. My parking space in the employee section is right next to one of those huge piles of dirty ice, and my foot slides down the slick patch. I grab on to the side of my car to catch my balance and mumble a curse under my breath.

"I guess breaking your ankle is one way to get out of this job." Ryan steps out of a red Jeep in front of my car. "But I wouldn't recommend it."

"Thanks for the tip," I say, and I make a face at him.

Let's hope he didn't see me talking to myself in the car like a crazy person.

"I saw you on the list of kids who have interviews at the job fair tomorrow. Congratulations." Ryan raises his hand, and I slap it. "With Senator Watson's office?"

I nod, feeling a fresh wave of nerves.

"You know you're going to do great, right?" Ryan says with an encouraging smile.

"Yeah. I got this," I say. Even though I don't know if that's true, I'm not letting anyone else know it.

Fake it till you make it.

Ryan grins. "You'll probably be some big-time political powerhouse in Washington, DC, one day, and I'm going to be cheering you on to keep raising minimum wage for me."

I can't help but smile back. He's being sweet. "I'm sure you'll be working for way more than minimum wage by the time I make it big in DC," I say. I look directly at him. For the first time I notice how his eyes are so dark brown, his pupils are only a slight shade darker. Suddenly, it feels like I'm staring at him and I glance away quickly. *Awkward.* This eye contact thing is harder than it sounds. But now I'm curious about Ryan's plans for the future. It's strange we've never talked about it.

"What are your plans after graduation?" I ask him as we walk toward the store entrance together, dodging the icy spots and parked cars.

"I'm hoping to go to vet school at CSU, but I'll probably start with an undergrad degree in biomedical sciences," Ryan says.

"Impressive." I remember his photographs on ChitChat. So he's artistic *and* brainy. Quite the combination.

Ryan starts to say something else but then my cell phone pings. I look down at the screen. It's an alert, telling me that I have a private message on ChitChat.

And it's from the TellTaleHeart account.

I freeze. My heart stops.

I thought this was over. But it isn't.

Ryan glances at me with a frown. "You okay?" he asks.

I manage to nod. "Go ahead without me," I say, my eyes glued to the phone screen. "I'll be right there."

"See you inside," he says, but his voice sounds faint.

"Excuse me." The woman pushing the shopping cart behind me is cranky that I stopped in front of her to look at my phone. I apologize. Then I look back at the screen, trembling, and open the private message.

TELLTALE♥: GOOD JOB. I LIKE THE NAILS. YOU FOLLOW DIRECTIONS WELL.

I reply quickly. YOU'LL DELETE THE SCREENSHOT?

TELLTALE♥: NOT SO FAST. WE'RE JUST STARTING TO HAVE FUN NOW.

No. No. No.
Before I can even respond, another message pops onto my screen.

TELLTALE♥: CHECK OUT MY ACCOUNT.

I don't want to, but I click over to the TellTaleHeart's ChitChit page.

It's no longer blank. In fact, there's a photo of someone's bare feet. My feet.

It's a tiny cropped corner of the screenshot.

And the caption under it reads: #staytunedformore.

So they're not bluffing. They're really going to post the screenshot.

I go back to our private conversation and type furiously.

ME: WHAT DO YOU WANT?
TELLTALE♥: LATER . . .

Later.

There is no time to reason with this invisible person now. If I clock in seven minutes late, I'll be written up. I race inside the store and jog down the center aisle lined with potted plants, floral bedspreads, and blow-up Easter bunnies. I unbutton my coat and fling it off, and start putting on my smock. The blackmailer will have to wait.

Someone's phone is ringing in the toy aisle and I quickly slide my own phone back into my pocket. I've been sneaking peeks at it all shift, but so far there've been no more messages.

The ringtone jangles on and on with some upbeat country-western song about trucks. Or tractors. Or trains.

I shift my weight from one foot to the other and scan the store for Mrs. Garcia. She's the manager on duty this evening, and she's stricter than Mr. King.

All I see is a kid kicking the end counter full of Maybelline makeup. She's probably about seven and is wearing a Superman sweatshirt. I don't think she's mad at the makeup. It's more like a very methodical task that she takes extremely seriously. *Kick. Kick. Kick.* A tube of lipstick rolls onto the floor and off toward the greeting card aisle. I glance around for an adult to tell her to stop, but there is no one in sight who looks promising.

Kick. Kick. Kick.

It's been three minutes since I last looked at my phone.

Suddenly, Mrs. Garcia appears at the service desk with her usual scowl. I've tried to cozy up to her on several occasions—complimenting the newly red tips on her black hair or her super-comfy-looking white sneakers or, that one time, her cool new hummingbird tattoo—but she never cracks. Today, she's even grimmer than usual, chewing ferociously. Gum took the place of smoking last year, one habit replacing the other almost seamlessly.

Chomp. Chomp. Chomp.

"If I see you with your phone out one more time, I'm writing you up," she tells me.

Oops.

"Sorry. It's just, there are no customers . . ." My voice trails off. I know it's a lame excuse. And Mrs. Garcia doesn't look like she's buying my apologies.

Chomp. Chomp. Chomp.

"Soon there won't be *any* customers." I should have seen it before, but now that I'm looking in her eyes I can tell Mrs. Garcia doesn't just look grumpy. She's worried.

"What do you mean?" I ask.

"The store is closing. Probably by the end of the month." She blinks rapidly, looking around to see if anyone is standing close enough to hear.

Oh my God. She's crying?

"Let's just keep this between us for now," she tells me in a low voice. "There's no need to get everyone upset yet."

I nod and she turns and leaves without another word.

I stand there, stricken. *What am I going to do if the store closes?*

I look around in a daze. What about Harmony and Ryan? And Millie Johnson, who works back in the paint section. She's like fiftysomething and has been here forever. But she's too young to retire.

I've been so selfish worrying about myself. A lot of the employees in this store depend on this job a lot more than I do.

"Do you have any stickers?" The little girl from the makeup aisle is peering at me over the countertop. Evidently, she's through with her assault on mascara and has moved on to other very important matters.

I look around for a parent, but still see no one. "No."

She frowns at me, brown eyes disappointed. "You should," she says, then turns to walk off toward the greeting card aisle.

I feel a twinge of guilt. I am the ultimate people pleaser, even when the people are very little. Then I check the clock. My shift is almost done. But tonight I'm locking up, so I'll be here for a while longer.

I sigh and make the closing announcement, watching as all the remaining customers slowly head to check out. The little girl in the Superman sweatshirt is being shepherded over to Harmony's register by an exhausted-looking mom. And the culprit with the annoying ringtone—a man in a cowboy hat—is purchasing a toy fire truck, probably for some grandkid.

When all the customers are gone, I watch as my fellow employees clock out for the night. Harmony is the last to leave. Afterward, I check the bathrooms for hideaway shoppers—none—and walk toward the front of the partially darkened store.

Now that I'm all alone, I can't keep the thoughts at bay. My mind bounces from one worrisome thing to the next.

The interview. The store closing. The screenshot.

A voice suddenly booms over the intercom, causing me to jump out of my skin.

"Attention, Kmart shoppers. Look up and look around for the bubbling blue beacon of bargain."

I'm not alone after all. It takes me a second to recognize the voice as Ryan's. I didn't know he was still here, but he often stays after closing to restock shelves.

I look around. Sure enough, the rotating blue light is flashing over in the toy aisle. It's a weird sight at this hour, made even brighter because most of the overhead lights are already turned off.

I follow the beacon straight to Ryan. He has a huge smile on his face and our biggest-selling drone in his hands.

"Help me test it out." His grin is now the size of a basketball.

"Are you crazy?" My smile is just as big. I'm relieved that my anxiety-filled train of thought has been derailed. Even if only for a minute.

"Probably." He winks at me. "Look, it's already out of the box," he says. "Besides, if we know how it works we can answer customers' questions, right?"

I blink uncertainly at him. "I guess so."

Playing with the toys after hours is definitely *against* the rules. Mrs. Garcia would not be happy. Even Mr. King wouldn't look the other way. I shouldn't be going along with Ryan's little scheme, but it's a way better option than obsessing over all my problems.

For once, I'm willing to take a risk on doing something unexpected.

Ryan carefully sets the drone on the floor. Then he punches a button on the remote control and the drone lights up. He looks at me with a mischievous smile and holds the remote out between us. I can't resist. I put my hand over his and we push the left button together. The drone lifts off the floor, straight up over the bicycles.

I scream, "Oh my God!" Then I cover my mouth, giggling at how loud I yelled. "Oops."

"Don't worry," Ryan says. "We're the only ones still here."

The drone hovers over our heads, waiting for our command.

"Hang on," I say. "I think someone needs to go along on this maiden voyage and report back."

Ryan raises his eyebrows in a question, but he brings the drone back to a bouncing touchdown right at our feet. "Got to work on my landings," he says.

I pick up a Barbie doll off the shelf. Some kids must have torn her out of the package and she's missing her tiny high-heeled pumps, but I figure she's good to go.

I carefully prop her up on top of the drone.

"Company?" Ryan picks up a slightly battered Tickle Me Elmo from another shelf. "Everybody needs a friend who makes you laugh."

"Perfect," I say, still grinning that goofy smile. I can't seem to get rid of it.

On a mission now, I run over to the hardware department and grab a bungee cord. All the customers who annoy us by taking items out of their wrapping are my best friends now. I hurry back to the toy aisle, where Ryan and I use the bungee cord to strap the passengers onto the drone.

"Time for takeoff," I say, giving Barbie's head a pat.

"Where to, Captain?" Ryan asks me.

"Since Barbie's shoeless, I'm thinking somewhere tropical," I say.

"Potted plants it is," Ryan says. "Shall we check in on the gerbils on our way?"

"Absolutely."

Ryan holds up his phone. "While you were over in Hardware, I downloaded the drone's app. Now we can see what the camera is seeing."

"Wow," I say. "You're committed."

Ryan smiles. "Very." He hands me the instruction booklet that comes with the drone. "You're in charge of navigation. We're on page three."

I flip pages quickly until I see the words *Operating Method*. "Push the left button to make it go up," I tell him.

"I already got that one," he says, pushing the button on the remote. The drone smoothly lifts off and hovers above us, Barbie and Elmo almost bumping their heads on the ceiling.

"It's working." Ryan holds out his phone for me to see the view from the drone. The whole store is visible from up there.

"That's pretty cool," I admit.

We glance up at the drone. Barbie slides off to one side and Ryan yells up at her, "Hold on!"

"Okay. Okay." I read faster. "Push up and down on the right button to make it go forward and . . ."

"Whoa!" Ryan yells. The drone zips off over the top of the assembled new bicycles and disappears toward the paint department. Ryan and I instantly lean over his phone screen to see a perfect overhead view of the linens department. With his free hand, Ryan pushes a button on the remote and the drone stops, hovering above an aisle of rugs and pillows.

Suddenly, from across the store, we hear Elmo say, "That tickles." The toy's maniacal laughter echoes across Women's Clothing.

I burst out laughing, holding my stomach and leaning forward. Through the giggles I finally manage to say, "You're going the wrong direction." I point toward the opposite corner of the store. "The gerbils are that way."

When the drone, the shoeless Barbie, a slightly battered Elmo, and the bungee cord are finally put back on their respective shelves, Ryan and I head outside into the night. I lock the doors to the store with Ryan waiting silently beside me. We walk toward the only two cars left in the parking lot.

"That was the first time I've seen you laugh all day," Ryan says.

"Sorry. I've just had a lot on my mind." *Understatement.* But for those few minutes watching Barbie and Elmo race around the Kmart sky, I didn't have a care in the world.

"No need to apologize," Ryan says. "Want to talk about it over some pizza?"

"Sure," I say, a little shocked at the invitation. "I guess so."

"Think the boyfriend will mind?" Ryan asks.

I'm surprised he knows about Luke. "Nah. Luke's not like that."

He steps off the curb and I follow. "How long have you guys been together?"

"Since the fall," I say.

"Long time," he says, and I nod. Suddenly, Luke feels very far away. Even though we hung out at lunch earlier today, I haven't confided in him about the screenshot yet. And I'm not sure I'm going to.

"He is going to study abroad next year in France. For this culinary exchange program." It feels strange talking to another guy about Luke.

"That's nice."

"Yeah," I say unenthusiastically. The word hangs there in the silence between us.

Then a voice comes out of nowhere. "You two are a little late locking up."

I jump. Harmony is standing beside my car in the dark.

It feels like my heart is going to leap out of my rib cage. "Oh man, Harmony. You freaking scared me to death," I say when I can actually speak again.

"What's up?" Harmony asks.

Awkward silence.

"We were going to get some pizza in Old Town," Ryan finally says.

Another awkward silence, longer this time.

"Want to come with us?" I ask. It's just a courtesy. I don't really expect her to say yes.

Harmony answers immediately. "Sure. I'll ride with you."

I mentally kick myself for being so polite, but there's not much else I can do. I unlock the passenger door and she gets in, slamming the door behind her. When I look at Ryan, he just shrugs.

"I'll follow you," he says.

I slide into the driver's side, start the car, and pull out of the space. Harmony is quiet in the seat beside me until we reach the edge of the parking lot.

"What's up with the Goth look?" She nods toward my hands on the steering wheel. Figures she would be the only person to comment.

Harmony is not going to intimidate me. Especially when she's in *my* car.

"According to *Vogue*, black is the color of elegance and sophistication," I tell her. "This color screams class."

I keep my left hand on the steering wheel and hold out my right hand, black nails proudly displayed in front of her face. Fluttering my fingers, I add, "I thought you'd surely know that."

Harmony's mouth falls open, then she bursts out laughing. "You got me good with that one." She holds up both her hands, fingers spread wide. I can see by the light from the streetlamps that her nails are black.

Harmony laughed out loud? I let myself crack a grin as

I make a left turn to join the traffic on College Avenue. In my rearview mirror, I see Ryan's Jeep behind us.

After a couple of blocks, we stop at a red light. The silence is heavy and I can't think of anything to say, so finally I ask, "Is Harmony your real name?"

"Yeah." I can feel the scowl from the seat next to me. "Everybody asks me that."

"Sorry," I say, because it seems like I should.

The light turns green. I push down on the gas and she surprises me by continuing.

"My mom used to sing backup in a band," Harmony says. "She moved around a lot. I was born somewhere between a gig at a steakhouse in Tupelo, Mississippi, and a county fair in Shreveport, Louisiana."

"And your dad?" I ask.

"He played the guitar in the band. I think he still lives somewhere in Mississippi."

"My dad lives in Texas now," I say. So Harmony and I have absent dads in common. Who knew? The tiny glimmer of a connection keeps me talking, trying to make another one. "My name comes from an island in Scotland. It's where my grandmother lived when she was a little girl."

"Cool."

I glance sideways at her, then back at the road. The drive up College Avenue means the scenery morphs from strip malls and chain restaurants into century-old brick buildings and million-dollar condos.

I sneak a peek at Harmony again. She's drawn back into herself and she's looking at me like I might have some dread disease. Now we're back on familiar ground.

"Yeah," I say. "The Isle of Skye. I'm going to go there one day."

"I'm going to go to Denver one day," Harmony says.

I laugh because I think she's kidding, but when I glance back at her face I'm not sure.

ASHA

In her dimly lit room, Asha sits on the edge of her bed, tying up the laces of her running shoes. For a moment, she thinks about climbing under her navy duvet and taking a nap before dinner. The covers are warm enough to tempt her out of her usual evening run, but she knows it isn't an option. She reaches for the phone and pulls up her running app. Yesterday she averaged ten minutes a mile. That isn't good enough.

No more avoiding the inevitable. She needs to get moving. Marcus Lopez is supposed to come by later and help her study for her math final exam. Maybe she should feel guilty for giving him hope she will go out with him if she aces the test. But he also said he was bringing Thai takeout, which will be yummy. And this way she can avoid having dinner with her parents in the main house.

Asha grabs her earbuds and heads for the door. Yesterday, she officially ended things with Nate via text. So who knows? If tonight goes well, maybe she'll let Marcus take her to a movie or something this weekend. At least he's smart enough to keep up with her.

She puts in her earbuds and turns her phone to her favorite running playlist. She slips out the door into the cold of the spring twilight. There is no wind, but her breath makes steamy clouds in the stillness.

Before she starts her route, Asha takes her phone out and looks into the camera, tucking a strand of hair behind one ear. She has her mother's eyes. Everyone says so. It used to make her feel proud, but now she doesn't know how to feel about inheriting her mother's traits.

Still, she takes a selfie and posts it. #IAmAshaMirza *running*.

At first, she jogs slowly, warming up. Her muscles respond and she runs faster, pushing her body harder. But no matter how fast her legs move, her brain moves even faster—jumping from one topic to another until it finally settles on Skye. It is a relief to think about something other than her mother. Even if it only lasts for the next mile or so.

Skye is upset about that stupid video. She never hides things well from Asha, but honestly that girl is too full of herself sometimes. Something needs to knock her off that pedestal.

Asha turns the corner onto the bike path on Lindenmeier Road, blood pumping through her veins. She decides to post some pictures on ChitChat of just her and Emma together, when she gets back from her run. She knows Skye will see them.

Obviously. That's the point.

Whenever Skye gets angry or doesn't want to do something, Asha just chooses Emma over her. That is the beauty of having two best friends. You can always play one off the other. And Asha knows Skye so well. She knows what will push her buttons.

Asha keeps running. Thoughts buzz around behind her eyes. Her body moves automatically, smoothly. Her brain, not so much.

Why is she even so annoyed at Skye lately? Asha wonders if it's because she wants Skye to pick up on what's wrong. She seems to have no clue.

It's like Asha isn't even important anymore. Like she is disappearing.

Asha adjusts her earbuds and turns up the music so loud that, for the rest of her run, she can't think of anything at all.

Later, she walks into the main house, sweaty and winded, to grab some Vitaminwater from her parents' fridge. On her phone, she tracks her route on the running app and uploads her time. Two minutes faster than yesterday.

Her breathing steadies and she swipes through her phone, selecting a cute pic of her and Emma from

Halloween. She posts the picture to ChitChat, caption-ing it #BFF and #memories.

She opens the fridge door to take out some Vitaminwater, then freezes.

Her mother's car keys lie beside the milk carton inside the fridge.

Asha steps back and closes the fridge door. She leans against the kitchen counter and puts her head in her hands.

#IAmAshaMirza *crying.*

CHAPTER SEVEN

SKYE

The Old Town part of Fort Collins supposedly inspired Disneyland's Main Street. I've never been to Disneyland, but that makes sense to me; all the quaint brick storefronts and colorful awnings seem Disney-esque. In the summertime, the square is filled with bands playing on the stage and children dancing in the fountains. In the winter, the Downtown Business Association sponsors the millions of tiny white lights decorating every branch in every tree to create a magical wonderland. It's spring, but the lights are still up.

In the seat beside me, Harmony is silent, arms crossed over her chest. I check the rearview mirror and see that Ryan is still behind us, which is comforting somehow.

I slow down and change lanes to avoid the clip-clop of a horse-drawn carriage full of hot-chocolate-drinking tourists. The evening crowd makes an empty parking space hard to find, so when Harmony points one out, I pull in quickly.

We get out of the car and wait on the sidewalk for Ryan, buttoning up our coats and slipping on mittens just in case he has to circle a few times for another open spot. But clearly he has the same parking karma as we do and joins us in only a few minutes.

The small pizza shop is jammed with college students watching an out of town football game on multiple television screens. The place is full of empty beer glasses and congratulatory yells and high fives, so I figure the local team must be winning.

"Let's sit in the back," Harmony says as she leads me and Ryan past the crowded tables and booths to a back corner. Ryan slides into the booth and Harmony immediately sits down next to him, leaving me to sit alone on the other side of the table.

"Where are you from?" the waitress asks Ryan, filling up our glasses with water.

He looks straight ahead. "California."

She tilts her head but doesn't ask anything further, leaving us with our menus.

"You know that's not what she was really asking, right?" I ask, when the waitress is out of earshot.

"Of course I know," he says.

"So why didn't you tell her?"

"Do random people ask you where you're from all the time?" he asks.

I shake my head.

He shrugs and takes a drink of water. "The question gets old."

I see Harmony giving me a look like I should have known better, and I realize she's right.

"Sorry," I tell Ryan, and he waves it off.

"How did the apartment search with your grandmother go yesterday?" I ask him, opening my menu.

"Not great," Ryan says with a sigh. "The newer places are way too expensive, so now she's talking about moving back to California to live with one of my aunties or, even worse, back to the Philippines." He frowns. "That will break my mom's heart."

"*All* places are too expensive," Harmony chimes in.

"Is your grandmother that unhappy here?" I ask, ignoring Harmony's random comment. "Maybe she'll get used to it if she gives it a chance . . ."

He shakes his head. "You know it's bad when all she sings are karaoke Elvis songs."

"Really?" I ask.

He nods but gives a half smile. "It's her go-to when she's really down."

Harmony picks up a menu off the table, then looks at me. "You're paying, right?"

"Okay," I say reluctantly, even though I think she's being completely rude and the bill is going to put a dent in my minimum-wage paycheck.

The waitress returns and asks, "Are we ready to order?"

Harmony immediately pipes up. "I'll have the extra-large supreme with extra pepperoni."

"You mean *we* will, right?" I ask her, exasperated.

Maybe we don't even like pepperoni. Did you think about that, Harmony?

"Um. Sure," she says. "*We'll* have the extra-large supreme, and add some jalapeños, too."

Ryan shrugs. "Sounds good to me."

"Me too," I admit. My stomach growls.

The waitress takes our drink orders, scribbling on the tiny pad of paper. Then she heads back to the kitchen, dodging the departing college students. The game must be over because the restaurant is emptying out quickly.

Harmony gets up to go to the bathroom and leaves me alone with Ryan. For a minute I feel awkward, hoping he didn't think this was a date or something. After all, he knows about Luke.

Our waitress brings us our drinks and I sip my Diet Coke while Ryan downs half his Sprite in one long gulp.

"I hope it's okay I invited Harmony," I say at last.

"Totally fine with me," Ryan says. "I think she's hilarious."

I almost choke on my soda. *Seriously? Are we talking about the same Harmony?*

I'm about to ask him for more information when my cell phone buzzes in my pocket. I take it out and glance at the screen.

It's a new ChitChat message.

TELLTALE♥: ARE YOU READY?

Not now. Not here.

I look up and scan the crowded restaurant. There are two sophomores I recognize from school hanging out in front of the televisions and a large family with three kids and a baby in a high chair over by the door.

Who is doing this to me?

My face feels frozen.

"What's wrong?" Ryan asks.

"Nothing. Just a text from my mom asking what time I'll be home." I glance back down at my phone, trying to make my face neutral. I type back.

ME: JUST STOP THIS.

A new message has come in.

TELLTALE♥: WE'RE JUST GETTING STARTED. NOW,
LET'S SEE HOW COMMITTED YOU ARE TO THIS
INTERNSHIP.

They know about the interview tomorrow. The thought makes me feel like the walls are closing in on me. Someone is inside my life, watching me.

Then I remember Asha's post about me and the interview that went out to everyone. How proud she was of me and my accomplishments.

But who would know how much this interview means to me? Who would care?

My heart is beating so hard it feels like it's going to pop out of my chest and go bouncing through the restaurant. Ryan is watching some commercial on TV, distracted, so I write back.

ME: WHO IS THIS?

Of course they don't answer my question.

But they do respond almost immediately.

TELLTALE♥: DRESS UP FOR YOUR INTERVIEW TOMORROW.

This time there is no hiding the panic when I look back up at Ryan.

Ryan puts his elbows on the table and leans forward, his brown eyes serious.

"Skye. What's going on? You're totally freaked out about something. Are you going to talk to me or not?"

I take a deep breath. I *do* feel like I have to tell someone. And Ryan is right here. Plus, it's obvious he's not the one sending me these messages. He hasn't had his phone out all night. Suddenly, I feel like I can trust him. It's just a gut feeling, but I go with it.

"Someone has been anonymously texting me and sending me messages on ChitChat," I blurt. "They took a screenshot of this video my friend Asha posted the other night and it's . . ." I pause.

The waitress is back with the pizza. We wait, silently, until she arranges it on a holder in the middle of the table and puts empty plates down.

"Everything look okay?" she asks.

Ryan answers quickly, still staring across the table at me. "Yeah, we're good."

When she finally leaves, he asks, "And?"

I continue. "They—whoever *they* are—sent me this screenshot of me, and told me to paint my nails black or else they'd post the screenshot online."

Ryan raises his eyebrows. "Is the screenshot *that* bad?"

I lift one shoulder. "Yes. I mean, kind of," I say, stumbling over the words. "I was being silly, dressing up in this nightie."

Ryan's mouth falls open and stays that way for a little too long.

I keep trying to explain, feeling myself flush. "It's just more revealing than I'm comfortable with."

I don't know if he's picturing it in his mind, or if he's shocked I would let it happen. Then he gives me a sympathetic smile.

"I get it," Ryan says through a mouthful of pizza. "You've got a reputation to uphold."

When he says it like that, I feel ridiculous and defensive. "Anyway, it's not about the photo. It's about the fact that someone is blackmailing me."

But it is about the photo, too.

"Okay, so you caved." Ryan nods toward my hands. "Your nails aren't exactly the end of the world."

"I know. I know. I thought it was just a stupid joke," I say. "But now they want more."

"Like what?" Ryan asks, brown eyes wide.

"I don't know yet." I push my phone across the table and let him read through the string of messages.

Ryan studies my screen, his brow furrowed. Then he hands the phone back across the table to me. I quickly click my phone to black, not wanting to look at it again.

Turning off the screen doesn't turn off my brain. The words and images are still burning against my eyelids.

"I'm sorry about this," Ryan says. "Have you told any teachers? The school counselor?"

I shake my head. "You're the first person I've told," I whisper.

"Really?" Ryan asks. "You mean you didn't confide in your boyfriend? Or your friends?"

I stare down at the table. This is a mistake. I could kick myself for spilling my guts right about now. Ryan chews on his pizza crust, waiting for me to answer. Finally, I do.

"I'm not sure who . . ." My voice drops off into silence and I bite my bottom lip. Finally, I add, "To trust."

Ryan nods slowly.

"The only thing I know is you didn't send the messages."

"How are you so sure?" Ryan asks.

"Because this last one was sent when you were sitting here."

"You know you can schedule ChitChat messages to be sent at any time, right?" he asks.

"I thought of that. At first," I say. "But you can't have a real-time conversation."

He considers this. "True."

"So it can't be you."

"But it could be anyone else," Ryan says, driving home the point that kept me from sleeping last night.

"What did I miss?" Harmony slides back into the booth beside Ryan. She tucks a strand of blonde hair behind her ear and gives me her complete attention, her eyes narrowed in concentration. I've never noticed before how deep blue they are—almost navy.

Suddenly, I'm aware of how long she's been gone. Had she already left the table when the message was sent earlier? I can't remember.

"Have you been messaging me?" I ask her. I can't keep it inside any longer. I hold up my phone with trembling hands and swipe the screen to show her the messages from TellTaleHeart. "Is this you?" I demand. "Just be honest."

Ryan glances back and forth between us, like he's horrified we're going to get into a fight. And normally I'd be too scared of Harmony to start any sort of confrontation. The girl takes boxing classes at the gym. But I feel like I have nothing to lose right now.

Harmony looks at me steadily. "No," she says. "I have no idea what you're talking about."

And just like that, I believe her.

All the fight goes out of me and I put my phone down.

"What's going on?" Harmony asks. She dives into the pizza, moving the largest slice over to her plate. She promptly scoops it up, folds it in half, and takes a huge bite, leaving a long string of cheese to dangle between her mouth and the remaining pizza. "What?" she asks, looking back and forth between me and Ryan.

Ryan laughs, handing her a stack of napkins. "Can't you eat like a normal person?"

"I'm hungry," Harmony says, still chewing. She swallows, keeping the rest of the slice inches away from her mouth and ready for the next bite. But first she asks, "So what is happening with you, Skye?"

I open my mouth and tell Harmony about the video Asha took of me.

"Yeah, I saw it," Harmony says. "So what?"

I'm shocked. *Harmony watched the video when it went up?* I know this should make me more suspicious of her, but it doesn't. She's clearly an honest person. And that's a relief.

"Why didn't you say something to me about it?" I ask.

She shrugs like it wasn't a big deal. "Why would I?"

Then I tell her about the messages I've been getting. It's easier to spill the whole story the second time around. Harmony narrows her eyes, focusing as though there is going to be a test later and she wants to remember every detail.

By the time I'm done, I'm actually feeling hungry again. I grab a slice of pizza off the tray and take a bite.

Harmony's eyes swivel from me to Ryan. He chews on a bite of pizza, neither of them saying anything. Finally, she breaks the silence.

"Do you have any enemies?"

I can't believe she's asking. "Seriously?"

She shrugs. "It's a question."

"Of course I don't."

Do I?

"That's what they always ask on *Law and Order*," Harmony says. Ryan looks at her like she's crazy. "I'm a big fan," she explains.

"I don't have any enemies," I say, and I hope it's true.

Harmony shrugs. "Then, sorry, but your friends have to be the prime suspects," she says bluntly.

My insides drop. She just stated my worst fear.

"They know a lot about you," Harmony continues. "Like, they know you have this interview."

"Yeah," I say, putting down my slice of pizza. "But anyone who follows me on social media knows a lot about me. It doesn't have to be someone close to me."

Ryan takes another slice of pizza for himself. "But I don't understand what's going on with the interview. You were going to dress up anyway, right?"

I manage a nod.

"Maybe they're going to try and make you blow it," he says thoughtfully. "But how?"

I shake my head. "It can't be good."

"You'll be okay," Ryan says. His dark eyes are so calm, I almost feel better. Even though the phone in my hand feels like a doomsday clock ticking down to some kind of explosion. "Keep us posted?" he adds.

"Yeah," Harmony says. "We can try to help you solve this."

I nod, feeling grateful. I hadn't ever expected to confess everything to Harmony and Ryan, of all people. This realization hits me like a ton of bricks.

Who are my real friends? I don't think I know anymore.

"Anyway." Harmony points to the last slice of pizza. "Are you going to eat that piece?"

"Go for it," I mumble.

To my surprise, though, Harmony doesn't eat the slice. She asks the waitress for a box so she can take it to go. I figure she'll save for it for a snack later.

When the bill comes, Ryan offers to split it with me, and I'm grateful. Harmony thanks us, but it sounds somewhat grudging.

I check my phone. No new ChitChat messages.

Outside, Harmony and I say good-bye to Ryan. He lifts his hand in kind of a salute, then heads off toward his Jeep. I stand there, watching him walk away, and feel my slightly improved mood leave with him.

"Do you need a ride somewhere?" I ask Harmony, and shoot her an overbright smile. She shakes her head.

"No, I'll walk the rest of the way." She turns and quickly heads toward the corner of Mountain and College. My car is parked in the same direction, but I have to practically run to keep up with her. We cross Mountain Avenue, Harmony in front, me trailing behind. Then she stops suddenly and I almost run into her back.

There is an older man bundled in a blanket on the bench. A pit bull mix is huddled at his feet, beside a sign that reads HOMELESS. ANYTHING HELPS. It is an all too common sight, but Harmony doesn't walk past like everyone else does. Like I would have done. Instead she squats in front of the bench, patting the dog's head and talking softly. If I weren't standing so close, I wouldn't have heard the words.

Harmony says, very softly, "Hey, Sweetie. Who's a good dog?" She takes something out of her coat pocket and holds out a bone-shaped treat on the flat of her palm. The dog leans forward, mouth open, and takes the treat very gently and slowly out of her hand, then chews it with eyes almost closed in ecstasy.

The man stirs and struggles to sit up, gathering up the blankets around him. "How you doing, Harmony?" he asks.

I'm surprised he knows her name. He looks over at me and I manage a self-conscious smile.

Harmony puts her box of leftover pizza down on the bench and pats him on the shoulder.

"You warm enough, Bennie?" she asks.

He nods and smiles. "We're good. Thanks for asking."

Then she keeps walking. Like it didn't even happen.

I follow behind her, and finally catch up.

"Is he going to stay out here tonight?" I ask her, gesturing back toward Bennie. "There's a shelter just around the corner. Maybe we should tell him."

"He knows." She shrugs. "But they don't take dogs. He won't go without Sweetie."

We stop beside my parked car. I don't know what to say in response. I wish I did.

"See you at work tomorrow." Harmony turns away and I watch her walk off toward the corner. I get into the car and am about to turn on the engine when I'm interrupted by the ping of a new ChitChat message.

The screen lights up and my world turns black.

TELLTALE♥: WEAR YOUR WINTER PROM DRESS TO THE INTERVIEW. THE PINK ONE.

HARMONY

The convenience store is empty except for the man and woman behind the counter. Harmony would have been surprised to discover anything different—and she is rarely surprised.

But there he is: the small, wrinkled pear of a man in blue overalls who always sits at the tiny metal table behind the counter, the *Coloradoan* spread out in front of him. Even though she doesn't know his real name, Harmony thinks he looks like Matthew Cuthbert, the character in *Anne of Green Gables* who gives Anne a home. The woman, who doesn't look anything like Harmony's idea of Marilla, sits at her usual place on a stool behind the cash register, her permed brown hair a fuzzy halo around her fleshy, scowling face.

Harmony nods in her direction, but there is no response.

"You didn't fill up the paper towels in the bathroom again," the woman says to Matthew.

No matter how often she's heard it, the venom in the woman's voice always makes Harmony cringe. She thinks again how there are some things worse than being alone. Yesterday the old man forgot to sweep off the steps—the day before that it was something about the ice machine. Harmony yanks open the cooler door to a blast of foggy cold air and pulls the Diet Coke out of the front space, watching tomorrow's drink slide down to take its place.

"How many times I got to tell you something." The voice carries clearly over the rows of candy bars and toilet paper.

Harmony picks up a package of powdered sugar doughnuts and heads toward the counter, trying to ignore the growing rage that never seems far from the surface these days.

The scowling woman behind the counter doesn't look up as she chants out the total: "Dollar thirty seven." Harmony reaches for her wallet.

"I do everything around here." The woman keeps talking in that same screeching tone, as though Harmony isn't even standing there in front of her. But they both know the woman isn't talking to Harmony, and the object of her anger, the little man behind the counter, simply turns to the sports page and keeps reading.

By now Harmony thought she might have an occasional conversation with the woman—maybe even just a word or two—about the weather or something in the news. But the woman never says more than that to her: "Dollar thirty seven." Never once looks up at her.

Then Harmony thinks she might make the woman notice her—say something—by doing something so outrageous that she would have no other choice than to acknowledge Harmony's presence. But then, just as quickly, Harmony thinks, *What would be the point?* She is invisible to the woman behind the counter, and to everybody else, it seems—except of course for the folks at the Kmart checkout counter who need toilet paper and toothpaste.

But then there's Ryan. And Skye. It was kind of nice, having dinner with them tonight. Hearing Skye's problems. It makes her suspect that Skye's life is not nearly as perfect as it seems. People's lives are complicated. She of all people knows this truth. When Harmony's mom hurt her back in a car accident last year, Harmony's whole life turned upside down. With no insurance and no way to make a paycheck as a waitress at Denny's, her mom's medical bills began to pile up quickly. Then the rent, utility, and food bills joined the growing pile and eventually swallowed them both up. Her mom got better, but they were so far behind it was impossible to catch up. They eventually gave up on crawling out of the mounting debt and just concentrated on the next day. And the day after that.

Harmony puts the money on the counter and leaves, untwisting the top of the Diet Coke and taking a long, caffeine-filled drink.

The glass door of the convenience store swings shut behind her on the woman's parting comment to her ever-silent companion.

"You hear me? I'm talking to you."

Outside, Harmony sits down at one of the pianos on the square. They've been painted by local artists and placed around town for the public to use. She picks out a melody, soft and haunting. Head down, she plays quietly at first, her fingers moving over the chords, stopping and starting again and again on one particular refrain. She waits for a moment, staring off toward the doors of the store, then starts playing again without pause. It's only when she thinks of the old man in the store that the notes come without a struggle. She wants to share how he must feel, trapped in a world so far away from Green Gables.

After she finishes playing, she takes a picture of the store and posts it to ChitChat. Then she checks in.

HARMONY HEAVEN IS WITH MATTHEW CUTHBERT AT WESTERN CONVENIENCE STORE.

When she leaves the piano behind, Harmony walks through the square and farther down Linden. She dodges some abandoned shopping carts filled with sleeping bags and discarded clothing from the Fort Collins Rescue Mission across the street. As usual, the Mission will be her final stopping place tonight, and she will meet up with her mom in a small room full of bunk beds and strangers in similar situations, but not now. Not yet.

CHAPTER EIGHT

SKYE

When I get home that night, all I can think of is the pink prom dress. I want to run straight to my room to look at it, but Mom is sitting at the table in the kitchen as I walk in.

"How are you?" she asks me, glancing up from her laptop. "Ready for your big interview tomorrow?"

If only she knew.

"Kind of," I say. "I just need to figure out what to wear." I feel a knot in my stomach as I say these words.

Mom rubs her eyes, then glances back down toward the computer.

"What are you working on?" I ask, hoping it will distract me from my problems.

"You're going to laugh," she says, the corners of her mouth turning down into a grimace.

I think about my day. "Probably not," I say.

"Two weeks ago, Paula said I needed to get a life."

Paula is my mom's best friend and coworker. She's my mom's age, but she dresses a whole lot younger—lots of eyelash extensions and fringy boho dresses.

"So what did you say?" I ask, sitting down at the table beside Mom.

"Well." Mom pauses and clears her throat. Her face reddens. *She's embarrassed*, I realize. "You know how she always wants to fix me up on a blind date?"

I hesitate. My mom hasn't dated anyone since she and my dad divorced three years ago. "And?" I finally ask.

"Paula dared me to make an online profile on that LoveBytes site and I did and then I posted it." Mom says all this in a big run-on sentence. Then she takes a huge breath, staring at me with a terrified expression on her face.

"Oh," I say, because I don't know what else to say. I never thought about my mom being on a dating site. Now that she is, I'm not sure how I feel about it.

I think about ChitChat. About the screenshot. Online, it's like the world is a huge apartment building with rows and rows of windows. For a few minutes, the shades snap open to reveal a carefully selected reality. And, just like that, the image is gone again, leaving behind only speculation and interpretation.

You have to be vigilant if you want to see everything. But no one really sees what happens beyond those windows.

Now my mom is opening up her life to new viewers. Crafting exactly what she wants them to see.

Some of the confusion must show on my face, because I see an instant flash of doubt cross Mom's.

"I'm going to delete it," she says, looking back down at the laptop screen. "It was a silly idea."

"No. It's okay, Mom," I say, mostly to make her feel better. "I think it's great for you to meet new people."

Her head comes back up. She runs her hands through her shoulder-length brown hair.

"Are you sure?" She leans in close and looks right at me, hazel eyes to hazel eyes. It's her secret way of getting the truth out of me. She used it when I was five and lied about stealing a coloring book from Mrs. Pratchett's kindergarten class. And she used it when I was thirteen and she asked if I was really okay with my dad moving two states away.

But I'm better now at hiding my feelings—even eye to eye. There's a quivery sensation in my stomach, but my stare is steady.

"Yes, definitely," I tell her. "You deserve to be happy."

I'm just not sure the internet is the way to do it.

My mom is forty-two and really pretty, even without fake eyelashes like Paula. But dating online will expose her to a whole new world of judgment.

Still, it *would* be nice if my mom could meet someone. I know it's been hard for her to raise me and my sister alone. It isn't her fault I feel a dad-sized hole in my heart every once in a blue moon.

"Who knows?" Mom says with a small laugh. "I might chicken out and take it down anyway." She gets up and walks over to the sink, running the water and splashing a little on her face. The red tinge fades from her cheeks with the cool water and she looks relieved.

"You should go on upstairs and get ready for tomorrow," she tells me. "You'll do great, I know it."

"Thanks, Mom," I say, getting up from the table. She comes over to wrap an arm around me, hugging me tight. It feels good.

Then Mom sits back down at the computer, her eyes on the screen again, and I leave the kitchen.

As I climb the stairs to my room, I wonder if Paula is excited about her matchmaking plan for my mom. My curiosity gets the better of me. I take out my phone and pull up Paula's social media account. After all, she's staged the window. All I'm doing is looking.

Paula's house is a mansion, something straight out of *Martha Stewart Living*. She has a hot tub. Her husband is an architect. Her daughter is going to medical school. Her son is a star tennis player at the private school he attends. They vacation in Portugal. And Jamaica. She's in a book club and has two cats—one black and one orange striped. There is a check-in at a winery in Napa and another at a Michelin-starred restaurant in New York.

Is my mom comparing her life to this? No wonder she thinks she needs a change.

I sigh and reach the second landing. My sister, Megan, is playing a video game in her bedroom. I can hear her and her friend Lulu, yelling at the screen over the sound of explosions and crashes.

Cassidy is waiting for me in the hallway, tail swishing. She follows me into my bedroom and slips inside the door just before I close it, jumping onto the corner of the bed.

Still holding my phone, I tumble onto my bed and bury my head in my pillows. Now that I'm alone again, the reality of the winter prom dress demand comes back to haunt me. Just when I thought the stupid screenshot game was over, there's this new hurdle.

That interview tomorrow is critical to my future plans, and someone out there in the big blue Galactic Network is trying to ruin it for me.

When I finally am able to open my eyes again, I roll onto my back, staring at the ceiling. Cassidy moves up the bed to lie across my stomach, head on my chest. My brain works furiously.

Who is doing this to me and how do I make them stop?

I try to think rationally, but every idea I come up with seems like a dead end as soon as I think it through. I close my eyes, tears leaking out of the corners of my lids and down my cheeks.

I know what I have to do. I roll off the bed and go to my closet. I pull the hanger out from the back and hold up the big poufy dress to the light. I study the short pink tulle skirt and scoop-necked, sequined bodice. This dress definitely isn't my style. It wasn't my style this past winter either, when I bought it for the dance.

Just seeing the dress brings it all back. The night of the winter prom was going to be the most romantic and triumphant night of my life. Student council had just held elections for the spring semester, and after a hard-fought runoff with Griffey Caro, I was named junior class vice president. I would be a gracious winner, twirling across the floor with my handsome boyfriend. Finally, everyone was starting to recognize my leadership potential.

The weekend before the dance, Asha, Emma, and I had gone to the mall together to shop for dresses. I tried on dress after dress, and couldn't find anything right. Emma was convinced we'd find my perfect look or die trying. Within the first hour, she'd purchased a white minidress that looked perfect on her model-like figure. I didn't have the same shopping karma, but then I never did. Asha, too, had found an off-the-shoulder purple dress that hugged her body perfectly. When she was done, she lost patience with my quest and went off to buy new running shoes.

Sipping on a McDonald's strawberry shake, Emma sat on the dressing room bench with one long leg crossed over the other, critiquing the last few options in my size. I was waffling between Emma's top choice—the pink, fluffy thing—and mine: a dark blue vintage-looking maxi dress with a beaded halter top.

"The pink one looks way better on you," Emma said.

As usual, I didn't want to disagree, but I wasn't convinced.

"I don't know. It's awfully short and very . . ." I turned back to the mirror, frowning. ". . . *very* . . . pink. It just doesn't look like *me*."

Emma tilted her head to one side and narrowed her eyes. "That's exactly the point. Do something different. Surprise people! Have a little fun."

So I bought the pink dress. Against my better judgment.

The day of the dance, I spent most of the afternoon at the salon getting my hair put up into a messy bun with carefully sprayed tendrils dangling down to brush my shoulders. At home, I paired the pink dress with silver strappy heels and sparkling earrings. When I looked in the mirror, all dressed up and ready to go, I hardly recognized myself. Maybe Emma was right. Different was good. If anything was going to solidify my new status at school, this was it.

I wanted Luke to be speechless when I opened the door—bowled over by my transformation. For once, we were going to be equals in the popularity game—hot jock and student council vice president in a great dress.

When Luke rang the bell, I ran to answer the door. There he was in a sleek gray suit with notched lapels and a red patterned tie. His shoulders were squared and his eyes were completely focused. *On me.*

"Wow," he said, staring.

I couldn't say anything at all. He was that gorgeous. I just tilted my head to look up at him and smiled. We were magic.

Strolling into the dance that night, holding Luke's hand, was like walking out onstage for a huge performance. Everyone turned to look at us and smile. We were high school royalty and I loved it. Finally, I was a winner.

But I soon found out it was all an illusion.

I can still hear the snarkiness in Griffey Caro's voice. She was standing with her back to me, talking to Luke, when I came back from the bathroom. Even the blaring music from the DJ didn't drown out her words.

"You know she only won that election because of you, right?" she was saying to Luke. "You're the popular one."

I froze, feeling my heart drop. I hadn't won because of my brilliant ideas for student council. A book drive for flooded libraries in Georgia. The home construction project for Habitat for Humanity. The welcome binder for new students.

It was about popularity. *Just like always.*

I didn't want *just like always.* I wanted better.

Luke never knew I overheard the conversation. He just knew I was different. When we danced together, it didn't feel romantic or triumphant. The evening suddenly felt like a disappointment, full of artificial costumes and unfulfilled expectations. And, no matter how hard I tried, things felt changed between me and Luke as he drove me home from the dance. It wasn't his fault, but now I knew *he* was my ticket to the political world at Rocky Mountain High School.

We said good-bye in the car, sitting in my driveway. When I kissed him good-night, our lips touched briefly and awkwardly, forced and unnatural.

Back in my room, I took the dress off and crammed it in the back corner of my closet, hoping I would never have to see it again.

I look at the dress now. It drips with disappointment and rejection. It's a reminder that I can't make it on my own without Luke or anyone else helping me. I can't wear it to the internship interview. It will taint everything.

Of course that's not the main reason I can't wear it. This dress wouldn't be considered professional in any situation, for *any* interview. But in this case it would be absolutely disastrous. Senator Watson is a strong, powerful role model who inspires women and girls to transcend stereotypes. She isn't about sparkles and pink. It would be an insult to her platform.

Then again, if the screenshot gets out, I won't even have a chance at another interview.

I yank the dress off the hanger and throw it over my desk chair.

That night I dream I am Abraham Lincoln.

I sit at the end of the reflecting pool in Washington, DC, watching the people climbing up the steps to stare up at me. I want to tell them to stop, but no matter how hard I try, the words won't come out. I need to tell them something important—something that will change their lives. But I can't. I don't have it in me.

Then they laugh. Hard. Asha is there beside them, pointing up at me and whispering words I cannot hear. The people laugh harder.

I can't move. Frozen in rock, I can only watch them looking and laughing at me.

The people are wearing brightly colored masquerade masks—blue, green, yellow—that just cover their eyes. Asha is the only one who doesn't have on a mask.

The better to see me.

I am Abraham Lincoln. I am huge. And I am wearing a pink, sparkly prom dress.

EMMA

Emma is holed up in a corner of the Old Town Library, working on her pitch for the screenwriting competition. There are only twenty-four hours left to write her entry and it is not going well. She's already written and deleted three different beginnings. She knows her idea is good. She just has to explain it the right way.

For some reason, it is especially difficult to focus tonight. And she doesn't even have the usual distractions of being at home. After dinner, she made up some excuse about going to meet Asha and Skye, and then drove to the library instead. Her parents barely pressed her on it.

Emma thinks about her parents, and it's like a huge black hole opens up in her brain. She hates the look that seems permanently etched into her mom's face—one of shame and betrayal. It's similar to the look Skye got when she realized Asha was filming her the other night at the birthday party.

Emma feels a pang of sympathy. Asha can really be difficult sometimes. She wishes she could vent about it to Skye. But Skye has been so busy lately. They all have their different obligations. It's not like when they were kids.

Emma focuses back on her laptop. She Googles the script for *Rear Window* and reads it through again. Then she puts in her earbuds and watches the opening scene frame by frame. Every few minutes, she stops and rewatches. Finally, she pulls up the blank page and starts to write.

CHAPTER NINE

SKYE

The next day, I spend an hour before school, my whole lunch period, and then another hour after school getting everything set up perfectly for the job fair. The rest of the student council helps, but I call the shots. Tables and chairs are all placed and labeled around the gym according to my design. I even put bouquets of fresh gladiolas and sunflowers on the tables for luck. Now I just hope everyone shows up and the event goes off without a hitch. After all, this is my biggest project to date as vice president. I can't afford any hiccups.

For the event, or for my own interview.

There is one more thing I have to do—get my interview outfit from home. After one more glance around the gym, I drive to my house with a pit in my stomach.

When I pull into my driveway, Luke is sitting on my porch in his green fleece jacket. He's wearing black sweatpants and a bright red stocking cap pulled low over his blond curls.

"What are you doing here?" I ask, walking up the porch steps. "I thought you had a soccer team meeting."

He holds out a plastic container and smiles. "I brought you some good-luck cookies. Not that you need luck."

You bet I do.

"Thanks," I say, opening the door for him to follow me inside. "I have a few minutes before I have to go back for the interview."

Once inside, we greet Cassidy, who barks happily. Luke and I peel off our jackets.

"You want something to drink?" I ask, my mind on the stupid pink dress waiting upstairs.

Luke shakes his head and settles in on the couch. He looks at me with his familiar lopsided smile and my heart hurts. He has no idea what I'm about to go back to school and do.

I have never rocked the boat, never done the unexpected. Now I have to do this one thing for myself and no one is going to make this choice for me—not Luke, Emma, or Asha. The blackmailer drew a huge mark in the sand of my life. I have to decide. Do nothing, or take a giant step over the line.

"You okay?" Luke asks. He reaches down to rub Cassidy's ears just where she likes it most.

"Yeah, why?" I ask, sitting down at the other end of the couch.

"I don't know." Luke props his long legs up on the ottoman. "You seem like something's bothering you lately."

"I have a lot on my mind," I say.

Trust him. Tell him about the blackmailer.

"So spill it."

Maybe I won't tell him everything, but some of it. I screw up my face, trying to figure out where to start. I've never talked to Luke about how I feel about myself. It's totally out of my comfort zone.

"I don't want to let people down." Even as I'm saying the words, they sound pathetic. "So I work really hard not to disappoint anyone. Not at school. Not at work."

Luke laughs. Not what I expected.

"Don't be silly," he says. "You can *never* disappoint anyone."

He is trying to reassure me, but instead it's like the bar just went up significantly. And I'll never measure up to it.

I give him a halfhearted smile. "Thanks," I say weakly.

I wonder if Luke doesn't really know me. If he can never truly understand me. Maybe that's why I haven't been able to tell him the truth about what's happening.

Luke checks the time on his phone. He has to go meet his soccer team, and I have to go upstairs and confront the pink dress. He gives me a quick kiss, and then he's gone.

*   *   *

I'm on my way back downstairs, wearing the stupid pink dress under my wool coat, when I run into Megan and Lulu. Megan immediately corners me and insists they have to go to Lulu's house *now*. Something about our Wi-Fi not working, and the two of them needing to watch tons of other YouTubers *right this second* to figure out their new channel. Even though I tell my sister I'm in a huge rush to get back to the job fair, Megan won't let up. So after lots of begging and drama, I give in.

Now Megan and Lulu are happily chattering away in the back seat, leaving me looking like an Uber driver up front.

An Uber driver in a pink ruffly dress that's hidden underneath her winter coat.

"Did I tell you we're going to launch our own girl gamer commentary on YouTube?" Megan asks me excitedly as I drive.

"Uh-huh," I mumble, glancing at the clock. "Only about a hundred times."

Of course the light up ahead turns red just when I reach the intersection. My fingers drum anxiously on the steering wheel. It's bad enough I'm showing up to this interview in my prom dress; I can't be late on top of that.

After waiting restlessly through two more lights, one four-way stop with three other cars that don't know how to take turns, and avoiding a mother pushing a stroller in a crosswalk, I finally clear the traffic for the final few miles to Lulu's house.

Lulu speaks up from the back seat. "Our YouTube channel is going to be smart, witty, and vastly entertaining."

"Where exactly do I turn?" I glance in the rearview mirror to catch Lulu's eye, but she's taking selfies, running her hands through her thick blonde hair and turning her head back and forth for each shot.

"Lulu?" I say.

"Just a sec." Lulu snaps a picture of Megan and then takes two more when Megan leans back against the car door.

"Hello? Can we focus?" I ask.

Lulu finally looks up from her phone and out the window. "Two streets up." She points. "Go right."

I turn into the neighborhood. Speed bumps are installed every few feet and are diligently monitored by an overactive homeowner's association, so I have to creep along at twenty miles an hour.

"Oh my God. Megan, you've got to see this," Lulu is saying. "It's this new app called FaceFix. It makes your selfies look better."

I peek in the rearview mirror. Lulu is holding out her phone to Megan.

"Here's the photo I just took of you," Lulu is saying. "Now I can use this eraser tool and make all your freckles disappear. Doesn't that look better?"

Freckles are bad? I've always loved Megan's freckles. Especially on her nose.

"Now let's use this brush tool and make your hair blonder." Lulu slides her finger back and forth across the screen of her phone.

"Now you hate my hair?" Megan asks.

"Hate is the wrong word," Lulu says hurriedly. "I'm thinking we just glam it up a bit. Not so . . . brown."

I pull into the driveway and put the car in park, waiting for the girls to get out. But they're still sitting with their heads bowed over Lulu's phone. Megan's brows are pulled together in concentration, her shoulders hunched up almost to her ears.

"See, doesn't that look better?" Lulu asks.

"I guess so," Megan says, a little quiver in her voice.

"And if you want, just choose this tiny check mark button at the bottom of the screen and it instantly replaces the old photo on ChitChat with this better one. Easy peasy."

"I don't want to," Megan says firmly. "That doesn't even look like me anymore."

"Okay. Don't stress. We'll take some more and play around with it. You'll get used to it."

"All right," Megan says reluctantly.

I want to say something, but I don't. The girls climb out of the car, and Megan thanks me for the ride.

"Let's take another picture," Lulu is saying to Megan. "You can stand over there and I'll take a full-body shot."

She points toward a tree in front of her house. "If you push your hips back, it'll make you look slimmer."

Her skin is wrong. Her hair is wrong. And now her body is wrong? Megan slams the car door behind her. I roll my window down.

"Have fun," I call out, but Megan doesn't answer back.

She follows Lulu up the drive, her back stiff. Watching her, my throat tightens. I pick up my phone and open ChitChat to write a new post.

SO DEPRESSED SEEING MY LITTLE SISTER LEARN ALL
ABOUT FACEFIX. DO WE REALLY NEED TO BE FIXED????

I hit share, then put my phone down and drive on to school.

The gym smells like stale sweat and buzzes with excitement. If I weren't so nervous, I'd be patting myself on the back for the amazing turnout. Everywhere I look are lines of résumé-carrying kids greeting polite, smiling recruiters.

Senator Watson's table is set way back in the far corner of the gym. I made sure it would be in a quiet spot away from the more popular tables recruiting for lifeguards and summer camp counselors.

I walk toward the table and take a couple of deep breaths to calm my jitters.

Then I sit down nervously on a gray folding chair positioned in front of the metal table and check my watch. It's just as bad to be too early as too late. A sign taped to the wall says someone will be with me shortly. My foot taps against the gym floor and I pull my wool coat in tighter around my body even though the heat is blasting through the floor vents.

Veronica Patterson is at the next table over, handing out flyers for lifeguard classes at the YMCA. The rumor is she's considering running for student body president senior year, and she would probably be my biggest competition if I decide to throw my hat in the ring. She catches me looking at her, tosses her long blonde braid over one shoulder, and gives me a fake smile. Suspicion nags at my brain.

Could she *be the one threatening me with the screenshot?*

Suddenly, I see a young man walking toward the table with one hand outstretched. I stand and shake his hand firmly, just like I practiced.

"Good afternoon," he says. "My name is James Scott. I'm the regional director for Senator Watson's office. You must be . . ." He looks down at the pad of paper in his hands. "Skye Matthews?"

Remember the to-do list. Smile more.

I give him a smile and nod. But then I blow it when my voice cracks on my hello. I clear my throat and try again. "It's so nice to meet you, Mr. Scott," I say.

"Please, call me James." He is younger than I expected,

with brown skin, brown eyes, and a head full of curly black hair. He's wearing a white button-down shirt with the sleeves rolled up and a loose red tie. "Please. Sit." He motions to my chair and I sit back down. "Would you like to get comfortable?"

I know what he means. I can't sit through the interview with a winter coat on. With great reluctance, I shrug out of my coat and hang it on the back of my chair, trying to ignore the queasy feeling in my throat.

This is it.

James pauses only slightly, taking in my outfit. I am sitting there, for all the world to see, in my pink prom dress. I hold my breath, waiting for him to say something.

He doesn't. He pulls out a messy pile of résumés from a leather satchel at his feet. He bundles the papers up into one stack, picks up a notepad underneath, and then pushes his tortoiseshell glasses back up his nose. He says, "If you'll just give me a minute, then we can chat."

I think that he could use some help with his office organization. Maybe I can work that into one of my answers?

I bite my lip, glancing around the gym while I wait. I see a couple of people looking my way, confused expressions on their faces. Veronica's BFF, Maria Salazar, is standing by her now. They are both blatantly staring at me. Their mouths are dropped wide open and flyers are frozen outstretched in their hands.

I look down, then back up. Two boys who are friends with Luke are standing over by the gym door, whispering and laughing. They point my way and pull in another boy walking by to share my humiliation. The one in the middle catches my eye and gives a loud whistle.

I know what everyone is wondering. *Why is Skye at an interview in her winter prom dress?* The whispers and stares swirl around me like clouds rolling in over the mountains.

The heat crawls up my neck. I lean forward to help my hair hide the red blotches on my throat that will surely follow.

James keeps flipping through the stack of papers, humming softly under his breath, until he finally unearths the one with my name on the top.

I watch as he scans my life, his eyes moving rapidly down the page.

How could he possibly know who I am by looking at that paper?

It's time to bring my A game. My eyes flick up to meet his, straight on, and I plaster on my best customer-service smile. All those hours at Kmart are finally going to be good for something. If I can handle Dead Goldfish Man, I can handle this.

To-do list. Lead with a compliment.

"Thank you so much for this opportunity," I say. "It's truly an honor. Senator Watson is such an inspiration."

James smiles back at me. Then he starts to recite what must be a well-worn spiel. "Our office has a competitive internship program for students, in both Senator Watson's Washington and Colorado offices. These structured internships provide the opportunity to learn about the role of a senatorial office and to be of service to our local community." He stops for minute and looks down at my résumé, then back up at me. "Now, tell me why you'd like to intern for Senator Watson."

I nod enthusiastically. "I feel like this internship will provide me with a unique opportunity to conduct policy research, attend hearings, write legislative reports, and respond to constituent inquiries at a local level. And everything starts right here in Colorado, at Senator Watson's home office."

That sounds good, even if most of it came right off the internship website.

"But you understand the job can also include some rather menial tasks, like answering phones, greeting guests, and even making coffee?" James asks.

"I would love to do menial tasks," I gush.

James laughs.

"I mean . . ." The heat is now in my face.

"I knew what you meant," he says. "So tell me a little about yourself, Skye." He picks up a pen from the table and writes a quick note on the top of his pad.

I start talking. I'm nervous, but the words come easily, no stumbling or pauses.

Just like you practiced.

"I'm a junior here at Rocky Mountain High School. I'm vice president of our student council. I work at Kmart, and I volunteer at Habitat for Humanity." I know nothing I'm saying is any different from what's on my résumé, but he nods and scribbles notes on his paper. His face is steady, his expression bland and unreadable. Unimpressed.

Talk about the senator's platform.

"I know Senator Watson is working hard to secure equal pay for equal work and make college affordable to everyone."

James nods, writing. While his eyes are focused on the paper, I glance around again. Then I see them: my besties. Emma and Asha are over by the basketball goals, staring at me with shocked expressions. Asha makes crazy circles at her ear with one finger and Emma's eyes are huge.

Quickly, I look back at James, trying to shut out the curious bystanders.

"Both those causes are extremely important for me, of course. To me." I fumble with the words, mentally kicking myself. "Because I'm going to college in a few years and I want to be able to make just as much as a man in the same job."

Duh. I should have said it more eloquently.

James glances over my shoulder—behind me is a constant hum of conversation—then back down at his pad. The clock on the wall is ticking down the minutes of my precious opportunity.

Change it up. Make him notice.

He's obviously ignoring the elephant in the room—the big sparkly pink one that I'm wearing. Maybe he thinks I think prom wear is business attire?

"You might be wondering why I would wear something like this"—I motion down to my disaster of a dress—"to meet you."

James looks up with a quick double blink. That gets his attention. He didn't expect me to deal with all the lace and ruffles head-on.

"Since you mentioned it, I was wondering. Your dress is"—he pauses—"nice, but . . ." His voice trails off.

"It's not what you'd expect to see someone wear to an interview," I say.

"True," he says. "We believe the appearance of interns makes a statement about themselves and about Senator Watson. They should conduct themselves in responsible manner, be courteous, dependable . . . and dress professionally."

"And this isn't exactly what you would call professional. That's why I wore it." My chin goes up. This is what I'd planned to do, and there's no backing down now.

"Not because I'm ignorant of Senator Watson's platform. In fact, it's just the opposite."

He raises his eyebrows in a question.

"I believe it's critical we stop judging a strong woman by the clothes she wears," I say, and I *can* say it easily, because I mean it. "Girls are given all kinds of mixed messages about how they should look and how they should dress." I meet his gaze. This could backfire in a spectacular way, but I'm willing to risk it. "You had an instant impression of me when you saw my dress, didn't you?"

James's face goes blank. "Perhaps," he says slowly.

"You might have thought I was frivolous? Or not very smart? Or too *girly* for this kind of work?"

"Perception and image are very important in politics, even if we don't like it. Femininity is a fine line to walk when . . ."

I set my jaw. *How DARE he?*

"Women make up only sixteen percent of Congress?" I don't drop my eyes. Now I'm talking off script, and it feels good. "Almost five times more men than women hold elected office in our country, yet women make up over half the population. That means we have over half of the skills, knowledge, and talents in this country and aren't able to use them to benefit our communities."

I stop talking, but the zeal is still hanging in the air between us.

"Well." James pauses, thinking, his long fingers tapping on the tabletop. I shift my weight on the chair. He is impressed. I can tell. "You certainly know how to stand out from the crowd."

Relief washes over me. "I'm a very hard worker, Mr. Scott, no matter what I'm wearing. I will do anything. I'll bring coffee, carry boxes, move furniture, and run errands. Whatever is needed."

My relief is changing to hope. I picture myself in the internship. I can almost hear the hustle of the people in suits racing up the steps to important meetings, votes and bills and hearings. And me, running along after senators, weighed down with books and briefcases. Eating takeout at a shared crowded desk in the wee hours of the morning. Debating policy and change with spark-eyed, like-minded dreamers.

"And all in a prom dress?" James asks.

I shake my head. "Of course not."

My brain is still spinning with ideas about my future. If I get this internship, it is only the beginning. Maybe one day I'll be in DC—in the shadow of the Washington Monument. At night, I will stand on the top step of the Jefferson Memorial and look out over the lights of the city. Maybe I'll whisper a secret into the ear of a stone soldier at the Korean War Memorial or toss a lucky penny into the reflecting pool. No matter what, I'll be there. Where it all happens.

"You understand, just like all legislative employees and volunteers, interns may be subject to a background check?" James asks.

"Of course," I say, beaming with my newfound confidence.

Then he adds one final thing.

"While interns keep their rights of expression as citizens, we're still going to want to check out your social media footprint. Since managing the senator's online presence will be one of the major responsibilities of the internship, we want to make sure you're up for the task. Do you have a problem with that?"

My mental celebration screeches to a halt. As much as I hate this stupid dress, it's nothing compared to that red nightie. I slide my hands into my lap and clasp them tightly together to stop them from trembling.

"Absolutely not," I say.

Ryan usually spends his break at work in a dark, windowless room across from the public bathrooms, alternately staring at a tattered paper sign on the bulletin board that reads "Human Resources Is Here to Listen" and scrolling on his phone. Tonight, however, he needs a breath of air that isn't tainted by Lysol air freshener.

He sits at the $29.99 plastic picnic table just outside the range of the motion-sensored Kmart doors and thinks about Skye. It seems strange to be here without her familiar smile, but he hopes things went well for her at the job fair. He pulls out his phone and his fingers pause for only a minute. Then he sends her a text.

RYAN: HEY U

SKYE: WHAT'S UP

RYAN: HOW DID INTERVIEW GO?

SKYE: UGH I GOT A NEW CHITCHAT MESSAGE LAST NIGHT. I HAD TO WEAR MY WINTER PROM DRESS.

RYAN: ???? TO THE INTERVIEW?

SKYE: YES

RYAN: SEND ME A PIC OF DRESS
SKYE: K

A photo comes through of a pink dress on a hanger. When Ryan looks at the photo, all he thinks about is how beautiful Skye must have looked on the night she wore this dress.

She is waiting for him to respond. He types something, then deletes it, then types something else and deletes it, too. Finally, he decides on a reply and sends it.

RYAN: WOW. SO HOW DID IT GO?
SKYE: LONG STORY. R U WORKING TOMORROW?
RYAN: NO. WANT TO TALK NOW?
SKYE: MAYBE
RYAN: MEET ME AT LORY PARK IN AN HOUR?
SKYE: ???
RYAN: WE CAN WALK AND TALK
SKYE: I KNOW YOU'RE FROM CALIFORNIA, BUT THERE IS SNOW ON THE GROUND UP THERE
RYAN: I HAVE SNOWSHOES ☺

CHAPTER TEN

SKYE

It is a beautiful afternoon for a walk, even with the big dinner platters—a.k.a. snowshoes—strapped to my feet. The air is crisp, but not cold.

I meet Ryan in the parking lot. He's wearing a red knit hat pulled low over his thick black hair and a long-sleeved soft gray T-shirt tucked into black snow pants. He stands up from buckling his snowshoe to his foot.

Cassidy is running circles around us both, excited to be included.

"Thanks for letting me bring her," I say, snapping her leash to her collar. I'd grabbed a tennis ball from my car. Now I slide it into my pocket to save for later.

"Are you kidding? I love dogs." Ryan reaches down to pet Cassidy's glossy brown head and her tail goes windshield-wiper crazy at the attention.

Cassidy looks up at Ryan, then back to me, smiling her panting, happy-dog smile. She knows she is the center of attention and she loves it.

From the parking lot, the snow-packed trail stretches out across the valley and then up the other side into a group of aspens, their white trunks speckled with black eyelike knobs. Beyond the trees are some of the highest peaks in the Rocky Mountains, stark jags of white ripping across the cloudless sky.

The intense sun is unexpected after the cold spell, but a Colorado spring can be surprisingly warm. Today is one of those surprises. Sunshine reflects off the snow, creating a sparkling wonderland. I blink, enjoying the warmth on my face, like a cat finding a sunny spot on the carpet.

All of a sudden, I feel strangely optimistic. The screen-shot business has been frustrating, but what real harm has it done? If anything, I've managed to turn it around in my favor. That stupid pink prom dress, now lying in a ball on the floor of my bedroom, holds no power over me anymore. It's just a shell.

"You ready?" I ask.

Ryan nods. "Let's do this."

I start off slowly on the trail, and I can hear Ryan crunching along beside me. Walking is awkward at first, until we adjust to the unfamiliar weights on our feet. There is no wind and no sound except for our breathing and footsteps.

There is not another human in sight. I let Cassidy off her leash and she runs ahead, circling back to check on us periodically, then running ahead again to sniff the ground and gallop about in snowy puffs of doggy delight. Every so often, she leaps off the trail and into the drifts, popping in and out of the snow like a seal. This time, when she comes back to us, her dark brown nose is covered with a dust of powder. I laugh.

"What in the world gave you the idea to do this?" I ask Ryan.

"I always thought it looked like fun in the movies."

"Doesn't California have snow somewhere? Tahoe?" I ask.

"Sure. I guess we just weren't much for winter sports in my family. I snowboarded a few times, but was never very good at it," he says. "This is much easier. All you have to do is walk."

"Yeah, it just takes a little while to get used to it." I look over at him and smile.

The sudden movement throws me off balance. I catch the tip of my snowshoe on the soft powder on the edge of the trail, and fall toward Ryan's shoulder. I twist my body, desperately seeking balance, and throw my hands out to keep the solid wall of white from rushing up toward my face. For a second, I think I might save it all at the last minute, reaching out to grab on to the one solid thing in reach—Ryan. But then we both go down in a tangled mess of snowshoes, arms, and legs.

When we finally get untangled, I can't stop laughing. Ryan is laughing at me laughing. So we lie there on our backs, snowshoes pointed toward the sky, laughing and laughing and laughing. Cassidy noses her way in between us, sniffing at our faces to make sure we're okay. The laughter slowly dies down, but we still lie there on our backs like spent snow angels, faces up to the sun. I look over at Ryan. He's just smiling up at the sky.

Ryan finally sits up, then stands—carefully negotiating his balance. He offers his hand, palm up, and I grab it, pulling myself to my feet. He helps set me upright, keeping one arm around my waist until he's sure I'm stable, and then we keep walking. I realize that in this moment, I'm not self-conscious about my size, or the way my breath comes hard when I walk, and that feels good.

Ryan says, "I thought you were the experienced one here."

"Me?" I laugh. "I've never been snowshoeing before. Despite being from Colorado."

He rolls his eyes. "So what good are you, then?" he teases.

"Fake it till you make it." I playfully punch his shoulder and waddle off in front of him.

"So how *did* the interview go?" he asks, when he catches up.

"It was almost a big disaster." We are both panting harder as we head up the hill toward the trees, our breath puffing out in white clouds of exertion. "But I was able to make it out alive."

I tell him about James's questions and my answers while we keep walking slowly up the hill and into a grove of bare aspens.

There's a stack of boulders in the sun and we stop for a moment. I sit on the rock and Ryan joins me, both of us soaking in the warmth.

"That's smart, how you handled the whole dress thing," Ryan tells me.

"Thank you," I say, grateful to have his support. I feel a flash of guilt that I'm not sharing this moment with Luke instead. But he's at his soccer team meeting. And it's not like I'm doing anything wrong. Ryan's just a friend.

"So what do you think about snowshoeing?" Ryan asks.

"Awesome," I say.

"I agree." He nods, then leans toward me. "You have a little something . . . here."

He reaches over, carefully tugging a twig out of my hair, then holding it out for me to see.

"Leftover from our nosedive earlier." Laughing, I brush my tangled hair back from my face with my fingers and dust the snow off the front of my jacket. I must look like a mess.

I glance up at the sky. The only thing to indicate there are any other people on earth is the white streak of an airplane across the cloudless blue. I think about how the sky, the sun, those mountains are all out of human control. But someone made that airplane. Someone is flying it right now. People are guiding it toward its destination and others will be waiting to lead it into the gate at the airport. Every person in every seat of that airplane is going somewhere, but they are passively waiting in their seats to get there.

I don't want to be buckled into a seat belt, eating small handfuls of peanuts and drinking from tiny plastic cups, with someone else in control of my destiny. I don't want my life to streak away under someone else's direction. That's exactly how the screenshot makes me feel—out of control. Even out here in the middle of nowhere, everything reminds me.

I pull the almost-forgotten yellow tennis ball out of my pocket. At the sight of it, Cassidy dances around my feet and I throw it out into the field in front of us. Within seconds, she's back, dropping the ball at my feet and waiting impatiently for the next toss. This time, Ryan picks it up and throws it. The bright yellow of the ball is easy to find, in stark contrast to the snow, but it's tough going to navigate the drifts. Cassidy leaps in and out of the snow, racing across the field at lightning speed to snatch up the ball. Then she's back again—waiting—the ball carefully placed at Ryan's feet.

"I have to warn you," I tell him. "You'll wear out before she does."

He laughs. "It's okay. I miss my dog. He died a couple of years ago."

"I'm sorry," I say. "What kind of dog?"

"He was a rescue. Part pit bull. Part something else. Smartest dog on the planet." He looks down at Cassidy, who has just placed the ball carefully between his two snowshoes and is waiting hopefully. Smiling, he picks up the ball and throws it again. "Present company excluded, of course."

I smile. "Of course."

Eventually, Ryan convinces Cassidy to take a break, but she keeps the tennis ball between her paws just in case. He pulls off his backpack and hands me a water bottle, then takes out one for himself. He carefully pours some of his water into a small cup and puts it on the ground for Cassidy, who laps it up. Then she stretches out in a sunny spot to pant happily.

"You're her new best friend," I tell Ryan.

"I think animals know when you're their kind of people," he says, and takes a swig from his water bottle. "I volunteered at the animal shelter back in California. I miss it."

While I drink out of the water bottle, he fumbles around a bit more in his bag until he pulls out a camera. He drapes the strap around his neck and fiddles with the buttons and dials. "I took portraits of the shelter animals to help them get adopted," he explains.

"You're a good photographer," I say, leaning back against the rock behind me with my hands clasped on top of my head. The heat from the sun seeps into my sweat-shirt. "I've seen some of your pictures online."

"Thanks. I'm trying to get better at landscapes." He lifts the camera to his eye and stands up to face the horizon, snapping a few pictures of Cassidy and the mountains beyond. "The rule of thirds."

"What does that mean?" I ask.

He pulls his camera down. "The sky should take up a third of the photo, the background the middle third, and the foreground the lower third."

I look back out at the valley with a new perspective. "So Cassidy is in the foreground?"

He grins. "Yeah. Do you want to be in the photos with her?"

I think about the beautiful girl who is in so many of Ryan's photos online. Amy. I shake my head. "I'd rather just Cassidy be the model."

I finish my water and hand Ryan back the bottle, thanking him for it. Then he stands up and takes some shots of Cassidy, and some of just the landscape. When he shows me the photos on his camera, I am impressed. My favorite is the one of a snow-covered pine and the mountains in the distance.

"The rule of thirds," I say, tapping the screen, and Ryan grins back at me.

"You're a much better student than my cousin Amy," he says.

"Cousin?" I repeat. I want to make sure I heard right.

He nods. "She lives in San Francisco. In my old neighborhood. She used to be my model for portraiture work. She was always wanting me to take pictures of her and all her girlfriends." He packs his water bottle into his backpack and puts the lens cap back on his camera. "But all she really cares about is looking good in the photo."

Amy is his cousin?

"She's gorgeous," I blurt, then feel my face growing hot. Now he knows I've been seriously checking him and all his friends out online.

He just smiles. "Believe me, she knows it."

I play with the zipper on my jacket, feeling self-conscious. "I wish I had her confidence."

I think of the screenshot and he must, too.

"You have no reason not to be confident," Ryan tells me.

I feel my face grow warm, and I try to explain. "Look, every time I go online, I'm slammed with hundreds of people who are prettier, smarter, richer . . . *better* than me. I can't help but think, *What's wrong with me?* And that screenshot? It brings all that into focus." My words come out more fervently than I intended.

Ryan frowns. "Well, the whole point of being online is to not to post anything imperfect. Instead everyone shows only the best parts, the edited version, of their life."

I feel bad because I know he's right. And then I feel

bad about feeling bad. Because I know that's how social media works.

"So on a scale of one to ten, if you had to guess, who do you think is blackmailing you?" he asks.

I take a breath. It needs saying. "Asha is about a seven, maybe an eight."

"Why?"

"She always teases me—daring me to do things outside my comfort zone. But it's not just me. She does it to everyone."

"Because it's funny?" His eyebrows draw together like he's trying to understand.

I shrug. "I guess." *Was Asha being funny, or just being in control?*

"Wearing that dress to the interview could have ruined everything for you. That's not so funny," he says.

"I know." I slide back on the rock, letting my snow-shoes dangle awkwardly above the ground. "When we were kids, Asha was so bossy. Always telling me what to do and where to go. Who to be friends with. What to wear. At the time, her shadow felt comfortable . . . sort of like a safety net."

"And now?" Ryan asks quietly.

I shrug. "We aren't kids anymore."

He turns toward me, pushing his sunglasses up on top of his head so I can see his eyes. "Why are you friends with someone like that?"

For some reason, that gets me. It's a question I've asked myself too many times.

"We've been friends forever. People expect us to be together."

I realize that's also how I feel about Luke. We've been together for a while, so people expect us to stay together. That's what makes being with him easy. But I realize I could never talk to Luke like I'm talking to Ryan now.

"Don't you ever do anything completely unexpected?" Ryan asks. "Like hang out with someone new . . ." He gives me this smile like he's daring me to do something wildly astonishing. "And different?"

I look at him. There is something between us—it makes my insides dance. I laugh awkwardly. "I thought that's what I am doing right now."

"Interesting," Ryan says, pulling his sunglasses back over his eyes. The grin stays on his face.

I look away from Ryan and back out at the field in front of us. The longer, sideways rays of the sun are softer now, turning the white expanse into crystal halos of light. Our tracks look like a giant rabbit hopped across the valley.

My voice is quieter. "I hope I'm wrong about Asha."

"For your sake, I hope so, too." He shakes his head like he's trying to clear his brain of a problem. "I left some good friends behind when I moved here. I miss seeing them every day, but they'll always be there for me."

"I guess not everyone who starts out with you in life will finish with you," I tell him. "Sometimes you have to let go of things . . . or people."

The sudden relaxing of his face could be anything, approval or understanding. I'm not sure. I stand up carefully, balancing on my snowshoes. Cassidy lifts her head, ears perked up and tongue hanging out one side of her mouth.

"We should head back," I say. "It gets dark quick once the sun starts going down behind the mountains."

EMMA

Emma sits nervously in the Lyric Cinema, along with the other contest applicants. They have submitted their proposals for their screenplays, and they're waiting to get feedback from Alexander, the head judge.

Trying to feel confident, Emma reminds herself that films about difficult situations are always winners. Conflict. Drama. Heartbreak.

Emma glances around. The theater looks different with the lights up. The seats are a little shabbier and the floors a tad bit stickier. Emma counts six other people spread out in the first three rows—her competition. Their ideas might be good, too, but Emma knows there is no one in this room who wants this more than her. And she is willing to do anything. Anything. To win that trip to New York.

To distract herself, she takes out her phone and posts a quote from *Rear Window* on ChitChat, along with a photo of the empty theater seats in front of her. Someday her movies are going to fill these seats.

At the front of the theater, Alexander takes a folder out of a beat-up backpack and the air goes out of the room. It's time.

Alexander speaks with a British accent, waves his hands around a lot, and loudly emphasizes key words. He holds up a stack of papers in his right hand and calls out across the room, "We shall *begin*."

Emma stares at the back of the seat in front of her, her chest tight with anticipation.

"Remember, film is *storytelling*. A powerful method for generating empathy and understanding." Alexander stalks back across the front of the theater, projecting his voice dramatically. "Your personality . . . views . . . ideas are going to be in this movie. There will be no difference between you and the movie. They are one."

He pauses and glances around.

"Okay. Who's up first?" Alexander asks the group.

A middle-aged woman with pink hair practically jumps out of her seat in the first row, racing up to stand beside Alexander like she is receiving an Academy Award. She gives her pitch: Her script will be a love story and her inspiration is *Casablanca*. Alexander tells her it has real potential and everyone oohs and ahhs in appreciation. Pink-haired woman practically dances her way back to her seat.

Emma drums her fingers against the armrests. Next up is a guy about Emma's age whose idea is a sci-fi script inspired by *Star Wars*. Alexander critiques it a bit, but then gives him a thumbs-up. Then there's a murder mystery idea, inspired by *Dial M for Murder*, another

Hitchcock movie. Emma hopes nobody else chose *Rear Window*.

Finally, it's her turn. She gets up and stands beside Alexander, pitching her concept to him and the other applicants.

"We're looking for *big* ideas, Emma," Alexander tells her when she's finished. "You have the basic concepts of an amazing plot, but I want to see *more*. If you want to make this script rise to the top, you need to amp up the internal emotional landscape. Make us *feel* it! We don't only want to see creativity in these short films, we want to see *real emotion*."

A lump rises in Emma's throat, but her face remains perfectly still. *Real emotion.* The last thing she wants to do now is show everyone in the room what her emotions are.

Feelings are something she's very good at hiding. She's had years of perfecting the art.

CHAPTER ELEVEN

SKYE

It's just after seven in the morning, and it's so warm under my covers I don't even want to stick my nose out of the blanket. I don't know why my mother will not turn up the heat! It's a constant battle between us—me turning it up and her yelling at me about how much money it costs.

I stretch one hand out for my phone on the nightstand and snatch it back quickly under my toasty little cover tent. The phone glows to life in my hand and I quickly search through all the possible windows for bad news. There's just the usual stuff: people posting about their homework or what they had for dinner or what movie they watched.

I have a text from Luke asking me how the interview went. I'm able to text back and honestly say it went well.

I went to bed last night feeling I'd somehow managed to pull off a good impression at the interview—pink dress and all. I should be happy. And I am. But there is this tiny little voice somewhere behind my ears that tells me this can't last. When one thing goes well, something else has to

happen to balance the karma out. You can't have wonderful forever. Everyone knows that.

No emails or phone calls from Senator Watson's office.

There are also no messages from my mysterious blackmailer. I fall back onto the pillow, closing my eyes in relief.

Finally, I drag myself out of bed and step over the pile
of pink dress on my floor on the way to the shower. There
is a nagging thought still roaming around my brain that
I can't shake. I told James in the interview that women
are judged too much on their appearance and image.
Yet I'm the one doing everything possible not to jeopardize
my image by letting someone share that screenshot with
the world.

The truth is I do care what people think of my image.

I'm a hypocrite.

When I get to school, I find Asha sitting on the floor by
my locker, books spread out in front of her Converse
sneakers. The steady stream of students flows around her
like water going around a boulder in the stream. She's
impossible to ignore.

Today she looks fierce in her Topshop oversized cardi-
gan and shredded Joe's jeans. Her thick black hair is pulled
up in a ponytail.

"Why should I even care about this stupid AP
Government test?" she wails when she sees me. "Don't

they know no one can concentrate the week before spring break? I give up."

"You're not a quitter," I say, which is definitely true.

Ignoring me, she pulls her phone out and snaps a selfie—positioning the phone to capture the most impressive view of the books in front of her. In typical Asha fashion, she must document every moment of her day—even not studying. It's like her life depends on her making sure everyone knows she is alive.

#IAmAshaMirza *stressed*.

"When is your test?" I ask.

She fumbles with selecting the best filters for the photo, her face buried in her phone. "Monday," she finally answers, then looks up from her phone and begs, "Take it for me."

That gets a laugh out of me. *As if.* "No way. I'm getting through next week, then spring break here I come."

Except I won't be snowboarding every day like you. My vacation will be spent working. At a Kmart. That's closing.

I take off my coat and put it in my locker. I dressed carefully this morning. My black jeans, black high-topped Vans, and black striped tee are as far away from pink lace as I can possibly get.

But it doesn't help.

"Hey, Skye. Don't you think you're a little underdressed today?" Will Johnson, one of Luke's soccer buddies, calls out from the top of the stairs.

His girlfriend, Melanie, leans against him and laughs. Her face is flat and round, with a turned-up nose and bow-shaped lips.

"Haven't you heard?" she says. "Pink ball gowns are the newest professional wardrobe staple."

Asha scowls at her threateningly, and Melanie holds her hands up in mock surrender. She says, "Even you have to admit it was weird."

Will grabs Melanie by the hand and they head back toward the band hall.

"Thanks," I tell Asha when they're gone. But she only turns her scowl on me.

"What were you thinking wearing that dress?" Asha demands. "You're the one who led that whole student council workshop last month on how to dress for your summer internship. Now this?"

I shrug my shoulders, but don't say anything.

"I don't think I even know. you anymore," Asha huffs.

The feeling is mutual. All of a sudden I want to cry. I don't trust her anymore and I hate it.

Emma comes around the corner then, wearing a huge smile. I feel myself relax. Emma always brings a feeling of peace. Today she looks like she just stepped off the pages of an album cover. She's wearing a felt hat and a short flowered dress with black tights.

"What's up, buttercups?" she asks me and Asha, walking toward us. She pulls a Burt's Bees lip balm out of her lime-green book bag and slathers her lips with clear gloss.

"Are you limping?" Asha asks Emma, looking down at her buckled, studded ankle boots.

"These boots give me blisters," Emma explains. "I haven't worn them in, like, forever."

"Why did you stop wearing them in the first place?" Asha asks.

"Because they hurt my feet. And cause blisters," Emma says.

Duh.

Holding out one foot for us to see, she adds, "But they're really cute."

Asha shakes her head in frustration. "Seriously?"

"Anyway," Emma says, ignoring Asha's scorn. "Not even blisters can bring me down. My pitch for my screenplay got approved!"

"That's great," I say, meaning it.

"Is this the *Rear Window* idea?" Asha asks, and Emma nods. I feel a flash of jealousy, that Asha knows more about Emma's project than I do. I guess I've been slightly distracted lately.

"What's *Rear Window* about?" I ask.

Emma narrows her blue eyes at me. "You've never seen *Rear Window*?"

I shake my head. So many things on my mind, but definitely not Emma's films.

"It's about this guy who is stuck in his apartment because he has a broken leg." She's talking so fast I can hardly keep up. "His window looks out over this courtyard and he can see in everybody's windows."

"So he spies on people?" I ask. "Sounds kind of creepy to me."

Emma shrugs. "It's Hitchcock. It's *supposed* to be creepy."

I pull out my math book and slam the locker door. I remember how I thought of the internet as a building where you can open your windows for other people to look in.

The screenshot. It's like someone just hit me between the eyes with a hammer. The idea that someone has the potential to share my life without my permission is horrifying. I rub my fist against my forehead, closing my eyes.

"Skye?" Emma asks me, touching my shoulder. "What's wrong? You've seemed weird lately."

I wish I could tell her. Instead, I close my locker, turn around, and say, "Nothing's wrong. Everything's perfect."

Because maybe it will be, right? Maybe the whole stupid thing is over and I'll never hear from my blackmailer again. Maybe I'll never even know who did it.

But this can't be all of it. They have to be building up to

something else. *What?* The thought hums inside my head like a constant buzzing I can't swat away.

Asha goes back to her books and Emma scrolls through her phone. I watch as kids pass by in the hallway. Friends. Classmates.

I make eye contact with Lily Eklund. Could it be her making me do these crazy things? Threatening me? We once had a competition in algebra over who had the highest semester average, but that was a long time ago. I can't believe she would still hold a grudge. I nod at her and she gives me a wave as she passes with a gaggle of her friends. Her smile seems the same as always.

Then there's Griffey Caro, working the visitor sign-in desk at the entrance. I can't forget the bitterness in her voice after I won the runoff election and the way she gave Luke all the credit for my win. Could *she* be the one behind this? I think of what Harmony said about enemies. If I had to pick one, Griffey might be the answer. Maybe nobody makes it all the way through high school without making at least one enemy.

I take a deep breath. I'm driving myself crazy with all this speculation. It's like a clock is ticking inside my brain until the explosion goes off and I don't know which wire to cut to make it stop counting down to annihilation.

Then I see Ryan across the hall, getting books from his locker, and I feel slightly better.

He lifts his chin at me. "Hey, Skye."

"Hi," I say, smiling back at him. I watch him close his locker and walk off toward the science hall.

"Who's that?" Asha asks me with interest, finally looking up from her textbooks.

"Ryan de la Cruz. I work with him. He just moved here from California last semester."

She glances back and forth between me and Ryan's retreating form. Then she puts her hand over her heart and squeals.

"Oooh," Asha says. "Looks like someone has a crush."

I feel my face go hot. She's baiting me, I know, but I feel like we're back in middle school and she's making me write a note to Jamie Cho asking if he likes me—*circle yes or no*. He said no, so Asha told everyone he stole her favorite notebook. When the teacher found it inside his book bag, I was never sure Asha didn't put it there herself.

I can't stand that smirk. I say, "He's just a friend."

Asha peers up at me, her brown eyes fierce with curiosity. "Maybe I should tell Luke about this *friend*?"

"Shut up, Asha," I say grimly.

She just makes kissy noises.

Emma says, "Stop teasing her, Asha."

"Whatever," Asha says, rolling her eyes.

When we were freshmen, Asha and I were put on opposite teams for dodgeball. Mrs. Peabody, the gym teacher, escalated dodgeball into a major contact sport before some parents complained. Asha quickly developed a formidable reputation for being completely ruthless. She could throw faster and harder than any other girl in class. Some were better than others at dodging, but most kids eventually got beaned by Asha's ball slamming into various parts of their bodies. She didn't care how pretty someone was or how popular, if she hated you or liked you. Where Asha was concerned, everyone was a target.

Even me.

At first I just hung out near the back line, letting other, braver girls stand in front. I was just waiting to be a victim. The only thing I didn't know for sure was how it *much* it was going to hurt. It all depended on whether it was a direct hit or a glancing blow.

But one day, for some reason I can't remember now, I changed things up. Surprised, everyone gratefully moved aside to let me step to the front of the cowering mass. Maybe they thought Asha wouldn't hit her best friend as hard as everyone else. They were wrong. But when Asha threw the ball directly at me with lightning-fast speed, I caught it. She was out. It surprised me more than anyone, but that day changed the way I played dodgeball. I never threw a ball, but I could catch one—no matter how hard it came at me.

I look at Asha now, sitting there as if she is a queen and the hallway her throne. She might be able to dish it out, but I can take it.

"Listen," I snap, jabbing a finger in Asha's face. "Stay out of my business."

Asha leans away from me in shock. Even Emma's mouth falls open.

The bell rings then, and I turn away from my friends and walk off. But I don't head to class. I hurry into the girls' bathroom. Within seconds, I'm in a stall sucking in air like I've just been pulled under the water in a riptide. I can't believe I lashed out at Asha like that, but maybe it was a long time coming. Maybe it's because I'm certain she's the one who took the screenshot.

Why would Asha do this to me?

But what if I'm all wrong and it's someone else? Then I must be hugely horrible, thinking my best friend might be such an awful person. And if it isn't Asha playing some warped joke, the person could be some kind of creepy stalker.

It has to be Asha.

I look up. On the back of the stall door is a scrawled message in black Sharpie about Jill Valencia.

Jill.

I shiver. I remember what happened with Jill. Her boyfriend shared her private pictures with all his friends last year. The boy was suspended, but it's not his name scrawled on every bathroom wall in the school. It's Jill's—with horrible messages and obscene tags attached.

"She shouldn't have taken those pictures in the first place."

"That's just the kind of girl she is."

This tag reads: *"Clap your hands if you've seen Jill's pix!!"*

Jill Valencia ended up transferring to another school, but her name is still here. Everywhere.

That could be me.

My phone buzzes.

I don't want to look at it. I figure it's Asha saying she's sorry. *No, Asha wouldn't admit she's wrong—not now, maybe not ever.* It must be Emma.

After forcing in a few more deep breaths and trying to calm my pounding heart, I look at the screen. It's a new ChitChat message. I freeze.

TELLTALE♥: YOU LOOKED LOVELY AT YOUR INTERVIEW YESTERDAY

The dingy white stall full of scrawled messages suddenly seems like a tiny cage. The Lysol smell makes me feel sick. My breath is coming in shallow gasps. I feel the fear fluttering in my heart.

Were you watching me? I want to ask. *Are you watching me now?*

I slide the lock open on the door and step out to the sink area, glancing around. The bathroom is empty. All the doors to the stalls are open. No one else is here.

Carefully, I put my phone on the countertop and turn on the faucet, letting the water run into the sink. There are tears pooling in my eyes and I splash some water on my face to wash them away. My mascara makes dark smudges under my eyes and, almost automatically, I reach for a paper towel to wipe it off. There are so many other things to think about right now, but I'm worried about what I look like? But if I didn't, none of this would be happening.

When I finish wiping my eyes, I glance back into the mirror. For a minute, I think someone else is standing there in front of me and she looks terrified. But no. It's me.

I look back at my screen—there is nothing more there—then back up at the pale face in the mirror. The girl in the mirror has no answers for me. The phone buzzes again.

TELLTALE♥: ONE MORE THING

My fingers tighten into a fist.

The door of the bathroom swings open and Harmony walks in. She nods at me, then stands at the sink beside me, pulling a hairbrush out of her backpack.

"How's it going?" Harmony asks, brushing her hair back into a ponytail.

"Fine," I say distractedly. I feel a strange waiting stillness inside even though my heart is pounding.

Whatever they want, I'll do it, and all of this will be over. I don't care that I'm already late to class. All I care about is waiting for the words to pop up on that tiny screen in my hand.

When they finally do, I reach out to grab the counter for support.

TELLTALE♥: BREAK UP WITH LUKE

With those four words, this horrible game changes. It's no longer about dresses and nail polish. Now it's about people. The ones in my life who matter. My eyes start to blur. It doesn't make sense. None of this does. Asha's always liked Luke and me together. Hasn't she? So maybe it isn't Asha. But who?

My hands shake as I type the same response that I whisper out loud.

ME: NO

"Are you okay?" Harmony asks me. Her voice sounds very far away.

This can't be real. I'm in a nightmare and can't wake up. Harmony is still waiting for an answer, her face crinkled in concern.

"Yeah." I stumble toward the door, my phone in hand. "I'll see you later."

The next message hits my phone before I even get out into the hall.

TELLTALE♥: END IT OR ELSE . . .

Then the screenshot pops up on my screen—the chubby girl in the tiny, Asha-sized nightie acting like she doesn't care if anybody sees her.

As if I didn't remember what the stakes are.

RYAN

RYAN: I SHOULD HAVE TOLD HER ABOUT THE
PHOTO.
HARMONY: THERE IS NOTHING WRONG WITH
IT. SHE LOOKS GREAT.
RYAN: BUT SHE DOESN'T KNOW.
HARMONY: YOU'LL TELL HER.
  . . .
HARMONY: EVENTUALLY

CHAPTER TWELVE

SKYE

Alleycat is a coffee shop tucked behind the major store-fronts on College Avenue. You go up a flight of wooden stairs, and the café takes up the whole top floor of the old building. The ceiling has oak beams and brightly painted tiles, with red walls and lime-green ceiling fans.

A tall guy with a curly ponytail and a hummingbird tattoo on his wrist is behind the bar pouring steamed milk into a large ceramic cup. He nods and smiles at me when I come through the door. I breathe in the smell of coffee and muffins.

I spot Ryan at a table by the windows, where he's reading a book and eating a blueberry scone. We're both off work this evening, so when I texted him to meet me here, he agreed right away. Normally, I might feel a little guilty about not hanging out with Luke instead, but Luke has soccer practice. Plus, I remind myself that I can't exactly go to Luke for advice about this latest demand.

"Hi," I say to Ryan, walking over.

Ryan looks up from his book. "Hi," he says, quickly

closing the book and pushing it into his backpack under the table, but not before I see the title.

"Tocqueville's *Democracy in America*?" I'm surprised.

He pulls the book out again, his cheeks turning a little red. "I saw you recommended it online. Thought I'd check it out."

He's reading Tocqueville because of me?

"Are you stalking me?" I joke.

He laughs. "It's on social media, so it's not exactly a secret."

I take off my coat and brush back my hair from my face, sitting down in the chair across from Ryan. "The wind is crazy out there."

"Haven't you heard, March comes in like a lion? You need something to warm you up. Mike's making me a vanilla latte." He gestures to the barista with the ponytail behind the counter. "You want one, too?"

"Sure," I say, still thinking about the book. Ryan gets up to grab us the coffees. When he comes back with two steaming cups, I thank him and then have to ask, "So what do you think about the book?" I try to sound nonchalant.

"It's slow going for me, but interesting."

I nod and take a sip of the hot drink. "Did you know that Tocqueville was sent to America from France to study the prison system, but he used his official business to study society instead?"

"To be honest, I haven't gotten very far," Ryan says with a smile. He sips his latte, too. "Promise you won't be disappointed in me if I don't finish it?"

I cross my heart. "I promise. I'm a total nerd for loving this stuff." But I am happy to hear that Ryan is at least interested in it all.

Ryan pushes the book across the table. "Enlighten me. What do you find so fascinating about his observations?"

If it's a challenge, I accept it. I pick up the book and flip the pages until I get to the section I want to read out loud. "This is what Tocqueville said about American women . . . *'She thinks for herself, speaks with freedom, and acts on her own impulse. . . . She is full of reliance on her own strength. . . . It is rare that an American woman, at any age, displays childish timidity or ignorance. . . . I have been frequently surprised and almost frightened at the singular address and happy boldness with which young women in America continue to manage their thoughts. . . . an American woman is always mistress of herself.'*"

Ryan grins. "Pretty smart for a French aristocrat living in the 1800s."

I think about how appropriate the words are to my current situation. It's like Tocqueville is standing there whispering in my ear.

Am I truly thinking for myself? Or is the person with the screenshot thinking for me?

I close the book and push it back across the table. I'm

about to tell Ryan about the latest demand from my black-mailer, but then he asks me another question.

"Why do you want to get involved in politics?" He studies me, sipping his drink.

I give myself a minute to consider. "Because . . . it impacts everything I can see from this chair." I spread my arms out, trying to show the scope. I feel the passion rise in my voice. "From the drink prices listed on the menu to the wages the guy makes behind the counter."

I break off and look out the window, down toward the parking lot below. "Like that woman out there walking with the little boy. Maybe she needs dependable childcare so she can work and support her family. Maybe she's walking because there isn't a good system of transportation in our city." I pause and turn in my chair. "And that guy over by the door?" I add in a low voice.

"The one in the red sweater with the bad cough?" Ryan cocks his head to one side.

I nod. "Maybe he needs to go to a doctor, but can't afford it," I say earnestly. "The government touches everything we do. And being in government can create real change. I want to be a part of it."

Ryan smiles. "You want to save the world?"

"Maybe not that," I say. "But I do want to make a difference."

"So I see why getting that summer internship is a really big deal to you."

"Yeah. I want to learn everything I can this summer, and next year I'd like to run for student body president."

Ryan looks impressed. "Sounds like you have it all planned out."

If someone doesn't ruin it for me.

I shove my hands into my hair, avoiding Ryan's eyes. Expectation is a funny thing. It can make you want to try really hard to reach that bar just over your head, or make you want to give up completely, daunted by the impossibility of it all. Right now my dreams seem like they are dangling just outside my reach and someone else keeps moving the bar higher and higher.

I return my focus to the latte in front of me and take a long sip. Suddenly, Harmony appears, sliding into the empty chair beside Ryan, with a mug of coffee in her hands. When she takes off her battered wool coat, she's wearing a black ribbed tank top. It's in stark contrast to her pale white skin, but it does show off the impressive definition of her upper arms.

"I thought you were working today," I say, surprised to see her. But I'm also surprised to not feel annoyed by her presence. I don't mind that she's here.

Harmony grimaces. "Mr. King let me go early, because I worked a double shift last night. I had to do all the price changes in Hardware before I left, though. Who knew cutting twenty-three cents off paintbrushes could be so difficult?"

"I hear you," I say. "I had to straighten up the wrapping paper aisle yesterday. People are slobs."

She groans and nods. "I needed some caffeine after that. Didn't know you guys would be here." She pulls a phone out of her pocket and starts tapping away at the screen.

Ryan looks at me. "Yeah. Skye wanted to meet because she said she had an update."

Harmony's eyes are bright and curious. "About the blackmailer?"

I sigh. "Yeah. I got a new message today."

Harmony nods. "I knew something was going on when I saw you in the bathroom at school."

"That's when the message came in," I admit.

Harmony holds up a hand, eyes still glued her phone. "Wait. Don't say anything yet. I want to check in."

I roll my eyes at Ryan, but we wait in silence, drinking our coffee, until she finally clicks off her phone and puts it back in her pocket.

"Okay. Go ahead," Harmony says, sipping at her steaming cup.

"The new demand is . . ." I don't want to say it out loud. "I have to break up with Luke."

"Or?" Harmony asks.

"Same as always. They'll share the screenshot."

"Whoa!" Harmony says. "This has taken a seriously dark turn."

"You're not going to do it, are you?" Ryan asks.

"I don't want to, but I don't see a choice."

How can I say that with Tocqueville's words still ringing in my ears? I feel completely gutless.

Ryan frowns. "You always have a choice. Is the photo really *that* bad?"

Yes, of course!

Is it?

"And what about Luke?" Harmony asks. "Don't you care about him?"

"I love Luke," I answer quickly, realizing I might sound a little defensive. "Everyone knows that."

Ryan shifts a little in his chair and takes a big gulp of his latte.

Harmony's eyes narrow. "*Why* do you love Luke?"

Who asks that?

But I find myself searching for the answer. "I feel like somebody special when Luke is by my side. People look at me differently. They treat me differently. They just *like* me more."

Harmony shakes her head like she doesn't understand. "But how do you *feel* about him?"

"Lucky," I say. "Grateful."

"That's not exactly mad, passionate love," Harmony says. Without asking, she grabs the scone off Ryan's plate and takes a huge bite, chewing thoughtfully.

Is Harmony right? Have I been with Luke all this time only because I'm *grateful* to be by his side? Did love never come into it at all? Yes, I always found Luke to be gorgeous. But did he ever make my heart flutter? Even when we kissed? I'm not sure.

I dare a glance at Ryan. He looks just as confused as Harmony does. And there's something else in his expression, too. Hope? Disappointment? I can't tell.

Harmony snaps her fingers like she just had a brilliant idea. "Maybe it's Luke who's been blackmailing you?"

"No." I shake my head firmly. "Luke would never do something like that to me. Besides, I was with him, at his house, when I got the very first messages."

"Yeah, and why would he want you to break up with him?" Ryan argues. "That doesn't make sense."

Harmony shrugs. "Maybe it's a test or something?"

"It can't be Luke," I say.

"Are you so sure?" Harmony still isn't convinced.

"I'm positive."

"Instead of breaking up with him, then, tell him what's happening," Harmony suggests. "I'm sure he'll understand."

My shoulders slump. "I don't know what to do."

Ryan shrugs. "*Ikaw ang bahala sa buhay mo*," he says.

"Huh?" Harmony asks.

"It's an expression in Tagalog. It basically means do what you want—you're in charge of your own life."

"Exactly." Harmony nods, and points enthusiastically toward Ryan. "What he said."

If only it were that easy.

"Who would want you to break up with Luke?" Harmony wonders out loud. "What about Asha? Has she ever been with you when any of the messages came in?"

I shake my head, searching my memories. "I don't think so. Which sucks."

Ryan and Harmony both look at me like they're feeling sorry for me. I hate that look. It was the same look I got from everyone when they found out my dad left.

My coffee cup is still half full, but it's grown cold. "I need to get home," I say. "Thanks again for the latte," I tell Ryan.

I pull my coat off the back of my chair and zip it up over my Fair Isle sweater.

Ryan asks, "You sure you're okay?"

I nod, heading for the door and down the steps to the sidewalk, but I'm not okay. Not at all. My hands are shaking with the buzz building inside me. People don't notice. Not yet. I can't focus on anything still. Everything is wavy and moving. My head feels like it might float off my shoulders.

Why is someone ruining my life?

I can't break up with Luke. Not now. Not like this. But if I don't, that screenshot will be everywhere. I'll be the laughingstock of the whole school.

I want my life back.

"Hey," Harmony says from behind me.

I stop and turn around to look at her. "What?"

"*Are* you okay?" Harmony asks.

"No," I say. "Everything is a disaster."

Harmony shrugs. "I get it. I'm not okay either. None of us are."

I'm startled. "That's not what you're supposed to say."

Harmony laughs and rolls her eyes toward the sky. "What do you want me to say?"

"Tell me everything's going to work out. That I'm going to be fine."

"I've got a better idea," Harmony says. "You want to work off some of that crazy?"

"What are you talking about?" I ask.

"I know a place. It helps me a lot. Come on."

The gym is closed, but somehow Harmony knows how to get in past the night custodian, who only nods and smiles.

Harmony and I take off our coats, boots, and socks and stash them in a corner. Harmony brings out two boxing gloves. Before she puts hers on, she helps me lace up mine.

Then she positions me in front of the punching bag. "Put your feet hip-width apart. Now bend your knees a bit."

I follow her example, putting my hands up on either side of my face.

"Pull your chin down. You need to protect your face."

I do as she says.

"First a jab. It's a fast, straight punch with your non-dominant hand." Her left hand shoots out and she pops the bag with a thud. "Now you."

I hit the bag, but the sound is much less solid.

"Keep your feet firmly planted. If your foot comes up, it will weaken the punch. Like this." She hits the bag again, hard. The sound of the thump echoes in the empty room. "You try."

I do, punching out and feeling my hand connect solidly with the bag. It feels great. I do it another time. And another.

"Good." Harmony grins at me. "Again. Harder."

I do it again. And again. And again. By the time I finally stop, the sweat is running down my forehead and I'm gasping for air. I lean over at my waist and try to catch my breath.

"Don't forget to breathe," Harmony tells me. "Now try a front kick. Like this."

She faces the bag, balancing on her back leg. Suddenly, her front leg shoots out, the ball of the foot connecting with the bag.

I try it. Not nearly as hard, but still a solid thump. It feels good. I do it again. I drop my fists at my side, wiping the sweat off my face with one shoulder and panting hard.

"Nice," Harmony says.

Tears come unexpectedly to my eyes. I blink them away. I didn't realize how angry I was until now. Maybe

I've been angry for a long time. Everything's been bottled up, and the lid pushed down on my insides is labeled, *"Be reliable. Be acceptable. Be perfect."*

And everybody knows perfect is a lie.

"Okay," Harmony says, stepping up beside me. "Let's try an uppercut."

We don't talk about Luke or the screenshot. Instead we punch and kick and sweat and breathe. I think of the bag as the blackmailer who is controlling everything. And when I do, I hit the bag harder and harder. It is my enemy—my tormentor—and this is my revenge. Harmony shows me how to do a side kick—and that feels even stronger.

I pound and punch every thought out of my brain until my hands tremble with the effort. Finally, I don't think of anything at all. My leg muscles burn, but for now my mind is finally quiet.

I walk over to the concrete wall and lean back against it, feeling the coolness against my skin. Sliding down the wall, I let my body collapse onto the floor, muscles spent.

Then I watch Harmony. Her body responds perfectly, just as it has been trained. Her hands and feet are so fast, they blur into the noise of the pounding. *Strong. Fast. Hard.* I can't help but be impressed. She is incredibly powerful.

When we're finally both exhausted, we towel off our sweat and change back into our boots and coats. Harmony thanks the night custodian, and we step out into the dark outside the gym. It's starting to snow again, the flakes big and slow-falling. My legs are still trembling, but I feel better than I have in days. And I owe it all to Harmony. Who would have thought?

"You're really a good teacher," I tell her.

"Don't sound so shocked." She looks different now—relaxed, happy, approachable.

"You're a much better teacher than you are a cashier."

"Ha," Harmony says, then actually laughs. "I don't like just standing in front of a cash register all day. I like being active."

"You should do this for real."

"You think so?" Harmony raises a questioning eyebrow.

I nod. "Fitness trainers make good money. Or you could be a physical education teacher. If you taught me gym, maybe I'd like it more."

Harmony smiles at me like I'm the best thing ever, a great big warm smile that completely changes her face into someone I've never seen before.

"How are you feeling now?" she asks, pulling her gray hoodie up over the top of her head.

"Tired," I say. I rub my eyes, then see the black smudges of my mascara on my fingers. My face must be a mess, but I don't care how I look.

"That's a good way to feel," Harmony says, then there is silence for a long time.

She finally breaks it. "Do you know what you're going to do?"

I shake my head, walking toward my car. "Do you need a ride somewhere?" I ask, my breath frosty in the cold air.

"No, I'm good. I can walk."

But when I drive away, she's still standing on the sidewalk, her face lit by the glow of the phone in her hand.

The post-workout calm is short-lived. On the way home from the gym I start to unravel again. I don't want to feel it, but everything starts to bubble back up into my thoughts. *Should I follow the blackmailer's directions and break up with Luke? What will happen if I don't? What will happen if I do?*

What will people think?

That question controls my life. I care about pleasing people so much, I am very good at ruling things out by asking that one question—things like what shirt to wear or how to style my hair or what color to paint my nails.

When we were younger, Emma used to always ask me why I cared so much about what other people thought. One day, in the sixth grade, she wore two different socks— one red, one green—to school. The audacity was shocking.

What will people think?

Emma laughed when I said that to her. She just didn't care. And, when the world didn't end because of mismatched socks, I wondered what it felt like to be so free of others' expectations.

I don't want to obsess over everyone else's opinions. It would make things so much easier to not care. But the possibility of rejection is a strong deterrent. The question haunts me.

What will people think?

My house is dark when I pull into the driveway. My mother and Megan must have already gone to bed. My body feels like a noodle and my brain is just as tired. I turn the car off and sit there, not willing to go inside yet. The snow is coming down harder now. It blankets the car, cocooning me inside. I close my eyes and lean my head back against the seat.

When I open my eyes again, I check my phone. I have a text from Luke saying good night. I don't reply. Tomorrow, I will have to decide what to do about Luke, and then live with that decision.

The Middleburgs' dining room table is at the front of the house and in clear view of everyone driving or walking by. Emma's mother never shuts the curtains when they eat, but then they are rarely at the table together. When they are, Emma feels like they are on display—the perfect family. Sometimes she wonders if someone out there watches them, making up a story about them. Like the main character in *Rear Window*.

Emma thinks of the movie again. Hitchcock's camera angles were all from the main character's point of view, so audiences actually saw into people's windows just as he did. That's exactly what Emma dreams of doing, once she becomes a filmmaker—showing people a different way of looking at things. And, best of all, Emma thinks, the audience will only end up seeing what she wants them to see—holding back those parts that do not fit into the story.

Tonight her parents do not fight. Instead, there is silence at the table. Emma picks at the roast chicken and moves the mashed potatoes around on her plate, her mind on the screenplay. She's been up late the past several nights, working on it on her laptop. It is almost finished. Just a few more edits. A cut here. A scene a little longer there. When it is done, it will be the first thing she feels she completely owns. It is her vision, her voice, and it is what she wants to say.

For once she has the power to make the world the way she wants it to look—not this horrible stillness, broken only by the clink of silverware against plates and ice rearranging in glasses. Finally, her father will realize she is serious about filmmaking and stop hounding her about her schoolwork. Finally, she will have an escape route from this house.

"Pass the mashed potatoes," her father says, breaking the silence. Then he holds up his water glass and shakes it to show it is empty.

Emma's mother jumps up, passing the bowl to Emma's father on the way to the kitchen to refill the glass.

For a moment, Emma thinks her father is a bit like Asha—entitled, bossy, and domineering. And her mother? A bit like Skye—always rushing to keep Asha happy, hidden in her shadow. So where does that leave Emma?

Invisible.

But not for long.

CHAPTER THIRTEEN

SKYE

The next evening, for the first time in a long time, we sit down for dinner as a family. Mom has brought home Chinese takeout and she opens cartons of kung pao chicken, beef with broccoli, and pork lo mein. Megan and I hurry over with plates and forks. Everything smells delicious.

On the table is a bouquet of fresh flowers, sprigs of baby's breath tucked into an arrangement of exotic mini-callas, daisy chrysanthemums, and yellow roses—my mom's favorite. The arrangement arrived earlier with a note that made my mom smile when she saw it, but all she said was that it was from a friend.

"Let me see the card," Megan begs now, but my mom slides it into the pocket of her jeans and quickly asks us to get extra napkins for the table. Megan shoots me a glance. I know we're both thinking the same thing, though.

Mom's blushing? Seriously?

I don't press it, though. I'm meeting Luke after dinner, and I want this evening to be as relaxed as possible.

After the three of us are done eating, we all reach for the fortune cookies. I rip off the plastic, hoping for some good luck for a change.

There's loud crunching from under the table and Mom says, "Megan, don't feed the dog from the table."

Megan doesn't try to deny it, but asks, "Want to know Cassidy's fortune?"

"Fine," Mom says, "but no more cookies. You'll make her sick."

Megan unfolds the slip of paper in her hand and reads aloud: "Someone is looking up to you." Then she giggles. "It's true!"

Megan nods toward Cassidy, who rolls her pleading brown eyes up to gaze adoringly at both of us. Or the cookies. It's hard to tell.

"No," I say. "*She's* the one looking up."

"So maybe she got your fortune by mistake," Megan says, glancing over at me with an exaggerated worshipful expression. "We're all looking up to *you*."

I study her freckled face and bright eyes. Guilt taps on my insides, reminding me of the screenshot, and what I'm about to do to Luke.

I don't deserve anyone looking up to me. Not even Cassidy.

"Open yours now," Megan urges me, pointing to the cookie in my hand.

I break open my cookie and read silently.

"Sometimes love isn't enough."

"What does it say?" Megan asks, popping the last half of an egg roll into her mouth.

"It's silly," I say, crumpling it up in my fist and shoving it into my pocket. First of all, it's not a fortune. Fortunes are supposed to say something like, "A mysterious stranger will bring you a million dollars" or "You will be going on a long trip." Second, it makes me cry because all I can think of is Luke and how people shouldn't put things in cookies that make you cry, just like they shouldn't put people in categories based on how they look.

I *do* love Luke. Or at least, I did. Maybe I loved the idea of him: this popular, handsome boy wanting to be with me. I think about how distant I've felt from him in the past few weeks, ever since I started getting the anonymous messages. Ever since I realized I didn't want to confide in him.

But is my love for Luke enough? I'm not sure. Luke is going to France next year. We may not even last anyway. Once that screenshot is posted online, it will be there on the internet for anyone to see. Forever. There is no taking it back.

My heart races, but everything else around me moves in slow motion.

"Are you crying over a cookie?" Megan asks, and I blink the tears quickly away. My mom looks up from her plate with concern.

"It's my contacts. They've been bothering me all day," I say, even though I took my contacts out before dinner.

"We should make an appointment with the eye doctor," Mom says, and I make a noncommittal sound.

"Lulu says I need to start wearing eye makeup," Megan announces. "Mascara, liner, shadow. That kind of stuff."

"Do you want to wear makeup?" my mom asks Megan, frowning.

Megan rolls her eyes. "It seems like a lot of trouble."

"Then there's no rush," my mom says. "You don't have to ever wear makeup if you don't want."

Megan sighs. "I don't want to wear makeup, but I do want to be friends with Lulu."

"If Lulu is your true friend, she won't make you do something you're not comfortable with," I say, and I wish someone would have convinced me of this back when I was in middle school.

Megan shakes her head. "You obviously don't know Lulu."

I shrug, and eat my fortune cookie.

When Luke comes over later, I meet him on the porch before he can even ring the bell. "Let's go for a drive," I say.

He looks down at me, a smile playing around his lips. My heart cracks.

"Where do you want to go?" he asks.

I clear my throat. "The park?"

"Your wish is my command," he says with a wink.

The crack in my heart widens.

I get in the car and Luke goes around the front to get in the driver's side. He starts the car and backs out of the drive. I glance at his profile out of the corner of my eye. *So cute. So familiar.*

How can I break up with one of the most popular boys in school? I'm the luckiest girl on the planet. And I don't want to hurt him.

But if I don't end things, that picture could hurt him, too. Embarrass him in front of all his friends. I can't let that happen.

Him or me?

Guilt crawls around in my stomach. I lean back into my seat, quietly watching the near-empty streets whiz by the window. A train whistle distracts me. It's far enough away to sound lonely. I remember being in the car with Dad, who always reacted to the trains in town with immediate action. The sound of the whistle was accompanied by a mumbled curse, then quickly judged for proximity. To beat the train crossing, and the long delay that would surely follow, we'd take off across town, turning this way and that, trying to miss any possibility of a blocked inter-section. Always listening to see if the train was coming or going, because direction is impossible to detect from just the sound of the horn. It's funny how a random sound can make you remember something. Or someone.

After a few minutes, Luke breaks the silence. "Everything okay?" he asks.

"Why?"

"Interesting. Answering a question with a question. You can't fool me. It's your classic way of avoiding something," Luke says.

"Sorry." In the darkness of the passenger seat, I bow my head and type on my phone, disengaging from the conversation.

> TO DO:
> SHOW EMPATHY. SAY, "ME TOO."
> ~~MAKE EYE CONTACT~~
> ~~LEAD CONVERSATIONS WITH A COMPLIMENT~~
> ~~SMILE MORE~~

Ten minutes later we're at City Park. Luke parks the car on the street and we get out. The snow is completely gone now, but it's definitely still cold enough at night for a jacket. I keep my gloved hands deep in the pockets of my down jacket and the bottom half of my face buried in a cozy faux fur scarf. My jeans are tucked into my Madden Girl boots to keep my feet warm and the sound of our footsteps is the only thing keeping my buzzing thoughts company.

I see Luke's breath come out in small puffs of air in front of his face. His smile is wide and trusting. He holds out his hand and I take mine out of my pocket to put it in his, fingers entwined. We walk up the grassy hill, hand in hand, toward a moonlit clearing at the top.

Luke pulls off his jacket and spreads it out on the grass. It's almost the same exact spot where we had a picnic last fall. It was our first real date and I was completely shocked when he pulled the picnic basket out of the trunk of his car. Inside were individual chicken pot pies, strawberry salad, and homemade cookies. I'll never forget how his lips tasted like cinnamon-dusted snickerdoodles.

Maybe it won't be a sound that reminds me of Luke. It will definitely be a smell—a whiff of vanilla or a hint of cinnamon.

Luke wraps an arm around my shoulders and I lean in to rest against him, just like I've done so many times before. Luke's eyes don't leave my face and I know he wants to kiss me, but he doesn't. Not yet. I look away, up to the sky, hoping for some kind of sign to make this easier.

The moon is almost full, and surrounded by hazy clouds of glowing light. While I watch, a white streak of fuel from an airplane taking off from Denver makes a perfectly straight line across the starry sky. It appears so suddenly—almost like some kind of message. I suck in air and hold it, waiting to see if there were will be another message. I need to know what's coming more than I need my breath, but there is only that one long white line and then nothing more. The airplane disappears behind one of the ghostly clouds to somewhere I've probably never been before. Nothing is going to make this easier. I start to feel sick to my stomach.

After a moment, I say, "Luke?"

He is smiling at me. "Yeah?"

"It isn't easy telling you this, but . . ." I stop and swallow hard, looking away. My eyes are filling up with tears and I can tell that makes him uncomfortable. His smile fades. I have to go ahead with this. I have to be brave. Finally, I say, "Someone is trying to blackmail me."

His forehead creases and he pulls away to be able to look at my face more fully. "What are you talking about?"

Now that I've started telling him, I have to keep going. "Asha and Emma and I were goofing around at Asha's slumber party and I tried on Asha's nightie. She filmed a video that was live on ChitChat and someone saved a screenshot. They sent it to me. It makes me look really . . ." My voice trails off. "Bad."

He laughs, almost like he's relieved the news wasn't worse. "Okay, so some random person sent you a screenshot. How bad can it be?"

"Bad enough to make me do things to keep them from sharing it."

I wait for him to ask to see the screenshot. When he doesn't, I give an internal sigh of relief.

Instead, Luke frowns. "What kinds of things?"

"Painting my nails black. Wearing my winter prom dress to the interview." My voice is shaky.

"Who's been asking you to do this?" Luke demands.

"I have no idea. I've been trying to figure it out."

"Well, it's all just silly stuff," Luke says, and shrugs, like none of this is a big deal. "Who cares what you wear or what color you paint your nails?"

"They just asked me to do something else," I say quietly.

"What?"

I take a big breath. "Break up with you."

His eyes go big and wide. "You weren't seriously going to do that, were you?"

I'm too quiet.

Luke stiffens. "Over a bad picture of yourself?"

"You don't understand, Luke. This picture is beyond embarrassing." I pause. "But listen. I have an idea. Maybe . . . we could just make it *look* like we broke up. Just until this whole thing goes away. We could spend less time together in public . . ."

I trail off. Luke's face has turned neutral; his jaw sets. No expression. I know this look well. It's his game face. The one he wears right before he takes the field in soccer.

"I'm not letting anyone intimidate us with threats," he says.

"Well, we'd still be together," I say, trying to make him

see. "But if we pretend we broke up, the person who's blackmailing me will leave me alone."

Luke rolls his eyes. "Just ignore this person."

"That's easy for you to say," I snap. Suddenly even through my anxiety, I start to feel a little angry. "You've never been made fun of. You've always been secure in your social position. And you have all your opportunities ahead of you already. That's not how it is for me. The screenshot could ruin my life."

"This is about the internship, isn't it?" Luke asks.

"In part," I say. "Someone from Senator Watson's staff is probably checking out my social media accounts right this minute."

Silence. He takes a breath. I face him, searching his face for a crack, an expression, an emotion. There is nothing.

Finally, he says, "Evidently, this internship is more important to you than I am."

"That's not true!" I protest. "Can't you just be supportive of me? I thought we could get through this together . . ."

More silence. I don't even breathe. Luke drops his head into his hands.

"Maybe we're just too different," Luke says quietly.

"What are you talking about?" I ask, feeling panic rise in me.

"You're so focused on your image." Then he meets my eyes. "That's why you've been staying with me this whole year, isn't it? I've been good for your image. Until now."

Is he right? Maybe a little bit? This is the kind of message I don't want to hear.

Suddenly, Luke stands up and starts to walk away. Jumping up to run after him, I feel light-headed. I grab his arm to stop him. "Wait. Listen to me, Luke. That's not true. I want us to be together. But this situation . . ."

"We don't have to pretend about breaking up, Skye."

My hand drops away. His arms are folded and he's refusing to look at me.

"What are you saying?" I ask.

He shakes his head.

"So that's it?" I can barely get the question out because I already know the answer.

He nods. "You can tell people whatever you want about who broke up with who. I won't say anything different."

It is like the ending of a movie I already saw coming. Luke and I have been existing inside a bubble that was always going to burst. We were never meant to be together. I didn't know how, but I knew this would eventually happen. And now it has.

"I'm sorry, Skye."

I start to cry.

Me too.

EMMA

Music plays loudly from speakers on Emma's messy dresser. She puts on bright-pink lipstick and smiles at her reflection in the mirror; then she turns off the music. There is yelling outside the door, but that is not a surprise. It is her father.

The words are punching bags. "You are such a stupid idiot."

"I said I was sorry. Why can't you just let it go?" Emma's mother begs. The dent in the Range Rover is something she couldn't hide. But it isn't her mother's fault. When she tries to explain again how it happened, the voices outside Emma's bedroom door get angrier and louder. And louder. And even louder.

There is a crash. Something falls over or someone throws something. It sounds like something that can't be fixed.

Like her family.

Like her.

Emma continues looking in the mirror without a change of expression. Outside her bedroom door, the yelling continues.

"Why would anyone marry such an ignorant pig? Look at yourself." Her father.

"Just calm down. You're right. I'm sorry." Her mother.

Emma isn't listening. Not really. Even though it is a constant noise, she has become used to it. Usually it is better to be invisible—to keep behind the scenes—than to attract her father's anger.

She opens her laptop and checks her email. There's a new email waiting from her aunt Karen in New York City. Emma scans it quickly:

> **If you can get here somehow . . . you are welcome to stay here anytime . . . getting your room ready . . . we're going to have so much fun . . . hang in there, sweetie . . . I know things aren't easy right now at home . . .**

Emma smiles. Her plans are coming together. Now all she has to do is win the contest. No matter what.

CHAPTER FOURTEEN

SKYE

The only time I leave my bedroom on Sunday morning is to feed Cassidy and pour myself a big glass of orange juice. Megan is spending the night at Lulu's and Mom is at work. The empty house is fine with me. I can't face anyone yet. My eyes are puffy and red from crying myself to sleep last night. After another round of sobbing into my pillow this morning, I think I'm all cried out for now. But I still feel sad.

Really. Really. Sad.

When I'm brave enough, I get down on my knees and crawl halfway under my bed to retrieve my phone from where I threw it last night. I look online, but Luke hasn't posted anything about our breakup. He hasn't texted me either.

No more Luke. No more going to his house for dessert tastings in the evenings. No more kisses that taste like vanilla. In school, I will no longer be the girlfriend of one of the most popular boys. I will just be plain old Skye again. I can imagine that it will be everyone's favorite new topic of conversation.

What did he see in her in the first place?

I want to call Emma and Asha. Maybe drown my heartbreak in Blue Bell cookies-and-cream ice cream like we used to do whenever one of us had boy drama.

But I don't. I can't.

A text pings onto my phone. My pulse races. I want to throw the phone back under the bed and climb under the covers, but I make myself look.

It's okay. It's just Megan. I take a couple of deep breaths.

MEGAN: CAN YOU PICK ME UP FROM LULU'S HOUSE?

I don't respond right away. Instead, I put the phone facedown on my nightstand and pull the covers up over my head. I close my eyes tight, willing Megan to go away. Another text. I push down the covers, roll over, pick up the phone, and look at the screen.

MEGAN: R U THERE????? PICK ME UP?

I sit up with a huge sigh and type back.

ME: NOW? WHY?
MEGAN: WE HAD A FIGHT. I WANT TO COME HOME.
ME: CAN YOU CALL MOM?

MEGAN: SHE'S AT WORK. NOT ANSWERING.
ME: FINE. GIVE ME 15 MIN.

Megan slams the door and sits silent in the passenger seat, her body stiff with anger. She's wearing a red hoodie, jeans, and Vans. It's hard for me to believe she'll be in high school next year. To me she's still just a kid.

"Do you want to talk about it?" I ask, backing out of Lulu's driveway. My heart's not really into solving Megan's problems. All I can think about is Luke's face last night when he dropped me off at home.

Megan doesn't respond.

I try again at the end of the street. "Did Lulu say something that upset you?"

"You wouldn't understand. You have plenty of friends," Megan mumbles.

I glance over at her. She has no idea. One of my so-called friends is a traitor. I force a smile. "Nobody has enough friends."

After about two blocks, Megan finally talks. "We were playing around with that FaceFix app again."

Her voice trails off and I wait for my turn at a four-way stop.

"And Lulu started telling me all the ways I looked wrong and how I should fix it."

"Like what?" I demand.

"She took off my freckles and made my teeth straighter. I didn't even look like me anymore."

There's a long silence and I can tell Megan's still stewing about the whole thing. She's never been that interested in her appearance before, but she's thirteen now and the pressures to look a certain way are starting to increase. Finally, she says, "There's nothing wrong with the gap in the front of my teeth. I like it."

"Did you tell Lulu that?" I ask.

Megan looks sulky and shakes her head. "I just told her I wanted to go home. Then I texted you."

"Don't let her bully you. Stick up for yourself." The words bounce around in my brain even as I say them. I need to take my own advice. "Don't get caught up in the lies on social media. Everyone shows only the best parts of their life. And, if they don't have anything good going on, they just make it up."

Megan's face crumples. "But you don't get it. I'm not popular like you, Skye. I only have one friend."

Popular? One friend is all it takes to ruin your life.

"You think it is easy being your sister?" she asks. "You're, like . . . perfect."

How could anyone think I'm perfect? I can't even stand up for myself.

But when I glance at Megan's face, I see truth. She idolizes me. The thought makes my hands tremble on the steering wheel. "Perfect is a lie."

"That's what Dad used to say," Megan says quietly.

I have a flashback to Dad sitting beside me at the kitchen table. I'm working on my algebra homework and frustrated I didn't get 100 percent on the last test.

"I just wanted it to be perfect," I said, sniffling a little.

He put his arms around me and pulled me into his side. "Perfect is a lie," he whispered into my hair. "Nobody's perfect."

My mind reels with the memory. "He said it to you, too?" I ask.

Megan turns her head and looks at me like I'm crazy. "All the time."

Then she looks out the window, her face hidden from me. "I think about him a lot," she says after a minute of silence. "Don't you?"

"Yeah," I say. "I do."

"Do you think he thinks about us, too?"

I want to tell her he does, but she needs my honesty. I say, "I don't know."

We drive the rest of the way home in silence.

Later that night, after everyone else has gone to bed and I'm sitting on the couch, flipping channels with Cassidy, I can't stop thinking about the stupid FaceFix app and the power of appearance. I turn off the television and make myself look at the screenshot again, the one the black-mailer texted me what feels like ages ago.

There are no filters or edits on my screenshot to make it look better. I suppose I could add those edits myself. But who decides what makes someone, or something, look better or worse? I don't want Megan trapped in the same chains as I am, vulnerable to some online bully.

Or worse, a best friend bully.

On Monday morning, Asha doesn't go to school. Instead, her family sits huddled together in the small, book-filled office of Dr. Martinez. Asha's dad holds a phone up so her older brother, Matt, can be present remotely. He couldn't fly back from his college in California for today's family meeting.

"I wanted to meet with you all today to check in on how you're doing. This is a very tough journey for any family. How are you feeling today, Mrs. Mirza?" Dr. Martinez asks, sliding her big black leather chair back from the desk and crossing her legs.

"Sometimes things that happened a month ago feel like last week." Asha's mom speaks very slowly and carefully, trying to group words together into sentences. Asha can tell that talking this way is exhausting for her, and there are long pauses, but eventually she finds the words. "Or I'll say something, thinking it just happened, only to be told I was talking about something from a year ago—or even longer."

It's going to get worse, Asha thinks.

"Like when I put the car keys in the fridge." Her mother stares at the doctor and her eyes fill with tears.

She glances over to meet Asha's stare and wipes the tears away quickly.

"We are not telling anyone," Asha's father says firmly.

Not sharing any of this with her friends seems wrong to Asha. But then true friends should know *something* isn't right. Even if you don't tell them. Maybe her friends don't care about her as much as she thought.

Dr. Martinez frowns at her dad. "Eventually, you will need help."

"Not yet."

The doctor nods like she understands. "Early-onset Alzheimer's disease is uncommon, but still affects at least two hundred thousand people under age sixty in the United States."

"Why us?" Asha manages to choke out the question. "Why Mom?"

Dr. Martinez gives her a sympathetic look. "We don't know why some people get the disease so early, but we do know there is a type that runs in families. When it is genetic, there is likely a parent or grandparent who also developed the disease at a young age."

"Both her parents died in a car accident when they were relatively young," Asha's dad says, putting his hand on Asha's mom's shoulder. "She never knew her grandparents."

Asha looks at her mother. There is a blankness in her eyes that was not there three months ago. It's like chunks of her life are torn out of her brain, leaving ragged, raw edges of images that she can't piece together—like a dream that haunts you with a glimpse of something just outside your grasp. The monster is getting closer, taking over everything that is her mother and blacking it out from the inside.

"Last week she got confused on her way home from the grocery store," Asha's dad adds, sounding more upset than Asha has ever heard him. "She had to call me to come get her."

"I understand your wife is still working?" Dr. Martinez asks Asha's dad.

He nods. "She can't lose her job now. I'm self-employed and her health insurance covers us both. It would ruin us financially."

Matt's voice comes from the phone. "Should Asha and I have some kind of test to see if we have it, too?"

Oh, God. Asha closes her eyes, breathing hard. The thought of a genetic time bomb ticking down inside her veins causes a fresh rush of raw panic to rise in her throat. *This could be my future, too.*

The doctor glances over at Asha's dad, then turns her full attention to Asha.

"You don't have to decide that now." Dr. Martinez's voice is calm. "If you want to consider it at some point, we can talk about the pros and cons."

"How do we help her?" Matt's voice seems so far

away. Asha wishes desperately he were here in person, not just some disconnected voice on the phone. There is a foggy blackness invading her brain that she can't escape. She needs someone—not Skye or Emma—to help her make sense out of all this.

"As I mentioned before, you can help your mother by moving as much of the mental processing outside her brain as possible," the doctor responds patiently. "Taking photos and filing them according to date can help give her a sort of bionic memory."

"I'm doing that," Asha says in relief. Finally, she feels somewhat helpful. Her voice breaks. "Every day. See?"

She takes her phone out of her bag and brings up her ChitChat page. There they are: the photos of Asha going about her day, all with that familiar hashtag: #IAmAshaMirza. Then Asha holds out the phone to her mother, watching her reaction carefully.

"Would you like to see some pictures?" Asha asks. "Mom?"

Her mother puts both hands on either side of the chair and pushes herself away from the cushion behind her. Leaning in further toward the phone, her nose almost touches the screen. She stays like that for a long moment, staring at the pictures with Asha sitting silently by her side. Finally, she pushes the words out of her head.

"I know you," she says, looking back up with a smile of relief. "You are Asha Mirza."

CHAPTER FIFTEEN

SKYE

At first, no one seems to notice the difference. Luke passes me in the hall and he nods, but keeps walking. I see the hurt in his eyes and it makes me feel horrible all over again.

Lunch is when it all starts to fall apart. Luke and I always sat together over by the windows, along with Asha and Emma. Asha is already at our usual table when I get there with my cafeteria hamburger and Tater Tots. At first, she's more interested in the Tater Tots, grabbing two and stuffing them in her face before I even sit down.

"Do you know how bad this stuff is for you?" she says with her mouth full. "You know I'm in training, right?"

"You could have fooled me." Emma joins us, sliding down the bench. She pulls the top off her blueberry yogurt and starts stirring up the fruit from the bottom.

"I forgot to bring my lunch," I say, staring at the food in front of me.

"Why is Luke sitting over there?" Asha asks, squinting at the far wall of the cafeteria.

Emma looks over her shoulder and starts to wave Luke over, but I stop her. "Don't."

Emma's brows wrinkle in confusion. "What's going on?"

"We broke up," I say, then try to take a bite of my hamburger. It tastes like cardboard and I chew forever before I can finally swallow.

"Who broke up with who?" Emma asks.

"It doesn't matter."

Bewildered, Asha asks, "Why didn't you call me?"

So you would know I held up my end of the deal?

"I didn't tell anyone." I swallow. It feels like the bite of hamburger is stuck in my throat.

Asha's eyes narrow and her face freezes. "Not even your *best* friend?"

The venom in her voice surprises me. I expected people to be surprised about my breakup with Luke. But why this raw anger?

Emma looks back and forth between me and Asha, but doesn't say anything.

"What am I? Nobody?" Asha stands up. Her voice gets louder. It's starting to attract stares. "Did you just *forget* about me?"

My head is spinning. I don't even know what to say. I remember how pouty Asha got when Emma and I wouldn't go snowboarding with her. How she was always so resentful of my job and the time I spent away from her. Did Asha decide to blackmail me because she was feeling left out? The idea makes me furious.

"Nobody can forget *you*, hashtag IAmAshaMirza. You won't let us. Every second of every day you're in our faces constantly reminding us of how *perfect* and *strong* and *great* you are." I spit out the words. The adrenaline pumps through my body like wildfire. "Just because you say it— over and over and over again—doesn't make it true."

"Calm down," Emma tells me, but I'm already standing up and walking away from the table.

"Wow," I hear Asha say from behind me. "Was telling me off on your stupid to-do list?"

Later, at work, I'm sitting outside on my break. I watch a woman push her cart across the lot at a snail's pace, a little boy toddling along beside her. He's drinking from a yellow ducky sippy cup and the mother stops every few steps for him to catch up. Across the drive, a man in a wheelchair lifts himself up and over into the driver's side of his van.

Earlier today, Mr. King told all the employees that the store was closing. A chorus of gasps and groans went up. Ryan looked startled, but Harmony looked the most upset of all. I wonder if this store has been a kind of home for her. I wanted to talk to her and Ryan about it, but then we all got slammed with a surprisingly busy afternoon. I'm grateful for the break now.

A single green leaf floats in a circle in the puddle at my feet. The sun warms the tips of my dirty black boots with the glow of late afternoon. I notice a smear of mud across the right toe. A car horn blares out at the stoplight.

It feels like everything is ending—my relationship with Luke, my friendship with Asha. My time at Kmart. But maybe it is a sign of new beginnings.

Summer is just around the corner. I want to believe in something good for a change.

Then a message buzzes across my phone. It's a new ChitChat message from TellTaleHeart.

I open it.

TELLTALE♥: YOUR SISTER JUST POSTED A PHOTO ON CHITCHAT.
TELLTALE♥: HAVE YOU SEEN IT?
TELLTALE♥: SHE'S PRETTY, BUT . . .

I blink. But what? Now this ogre is coming for my sister, too? Every protective nerve in my body starts to tingle.

TELLTALE♥: I'M SURE SHE WANTS TO LOOK EVEN BETTER.
TELLTALE♥: WHY DON'T YOU FACEFIX IT?
TELLTALE♥: OR ELSE, WELL, YOU KNOW . . .

The rage bubbles into my shaking hands as I pull up Megan's ChitChat page. I look at the photo she just posted.

She is in our house, bent over and hugging Cassidy, and smiling at the camera. No makeup. No filters. No alterations. Just vibrant happiness. There is nothing there I want to fix. It is pure and perfect just as it is.

Something snaps in my brain. It has been a long time coming and a lot was lost along the way, but the line is finally crossed. Megan will not be a sacrifice to this Galactic Network of lies and intimidations.

ME: NO

TELLTALE♥: REALLY? YOU KNOW WHAT'S AT STAKE . . .

I do. I pull up the screenshot on my phone and stare at it for a very long time. The image I hold in my hand is what's been driving me crazy and making me a prisoner. *Of what?*

For the first time, I really see the image. The girl in the photo looks . . . pretty. Her smile is wide and free. Her bare shoulders are round—maybe too soft by some people's standards—but lovely just as they are. Hazel eyes are crinkled with laughter. Thick light-brown hair is big and wild and fun. She is me—unaware of other people's eyes and judgment for once in her life. She's not posing for anyone.

She's not perfect, but she's real.

I was lost so deep in this one superficial image, I was willing to do almost anything. I couldn't bear letting the outside world see a different me than the one I so carefully created.

The walls of my identity waver. Start to crumble. Can I be the person in the photo and still be me?

Why does it matter what other people think?

An idea creeps into my head. One I can hardly believe I'm considering. Tears slide down my face. I hesitate. There is something I need to do, and it's not on some likability list. My to-do list was about what I lacked. My shortcomings. But I didn't need to do *more* things, I need to do things that truly matter. Important things. Like this. It's my choice to take back my life. I am the one calling the shots.

My message back is short.

ME: I'M TAKING AWAY YOUR POWER.

Then I post the screenshot onto my ChitChat page. With shaking fingers, I hit *Share*.

And it goes everywhere.

"How are you doing?" Asha's dad asks, sitting down on the edge of her bed that evening.

Asha puts down her phone. "I've been better."

"Me too."

"What are we going to do?" Asha asks. It's a much bigger question than here and now.

"I don't know." Her dad has a half smile on his face, shaking his head slightly. His brown eyes are sad. "But we'll get through this somehow. Together."

Asha wipes her tears on the back of her hand.

Her dad hesitates. "The doctor is right. It's time for us to start talking about this and get some help. I was wrong to ask you to keep your mom's illness a secret. You need your friends' support."

It feels like a gift. "Are you sure?" Asha asks softly.

He nods, solemnly, puts his arm around her, and pulls her in for a tight hug.

After her dad leaves, Asha changes into an over-sized T-shirt and washes off her makeup. She sits cross-legged on her bed, opens her laptop, and plugs in her headphones. But before she starts her homework, she checks into ChitChat and her fingers freeze on the keyboard.

Skye's screenshot fills the screen. Asha claps a hand over her mouth with a gasp.

Why would she post this? This was never supposed to happen!

CHAPTER SIXTEEN

SKYE

It's the day before Spring Break—it starts on a Wednesday this year—but nobody's talking about the upcoming vacation. Instead, they are all whispering and pointing at me. Even though I try to walk with my head held high, I hear the comments in the halls. I now know the answer to the question *What will people think?*—and it isn't anything good.

"Why would she post a picture of herself like *that*?"

"Obviously, she thinks she's hot."

"Ewwwwww."

First period is excruciating. Emma makes a gesture, pointing at her phone. I've had mine turned off since I posted the screenshot last night, but I pull it out from my backpack now, keeping it under my desk. I turn it on to see Emma's texts.

EMMA: ARE YOU OKAY?????

EMMA: JUST IGNORE THEM!

I turn the phone off again and put it into my book bag, not looking at anything or anyone else. I stare straight down at my textbook, willing Mr. Sample, the math teacher, to start class on time for once. Instead he stands at the door, talking to Mrs. Drager about collecting money for some other teacher's birthday cake.

Beside me, Asha taps away at her phone, and a minute later Emma's phone pings. Asha nods vigorously at Emma and I'm sure they're texting about me.

Mr. Sample walks to his desk and I feel relieved, but then he just digs around in his desk for some cash and goes back to the door. My hopes sink.

The boys behind me are laughing so loud they don't even try to hide it. I know they are laughing at me. Someone throws a wadded-up piece of paper at me. It bounces off my arm and lies there on my desk. Even though I know people are watching, I straighten the piece of paper out. It's a drawing of a cow in a bikini. There's a big red lip print over the face.

I can't breathe. *How stupid could I be?*

Even if the attention eventually moves on, that screenshot will be on the internet forever. All my confidence from last night has disappeared. This decision will cost me everything. My insides crawl from the reality of this public scrutiny. I may have taken control of my life back, but the consequences of doing so are real.

I feel Asha staring at me. I try to ignore her frantic gaze, but she kicks the leg of my chair to make me look at her. She leans across the aisle to snatch the cow picture from my desk and crumples it into a tight ball with one fist. Then she glares at the boys. They shut up.

"*Why?*" she mouths at me. She looks so confused. I'm sure she's frustrated I ended her stupid game. If I didn't know what she'd done, I'd almost feel sorry for her.

You know why I shared that screenshot, Asha. You're the only one who does.

Mr. Sample finally comes back in the room to take roll. When he gets to my name, he looks at me like he's so disappointed. I'm sure by now someone has shared the screenshot with him.

"Skye, would you like to go to the counselor's office?" he asks.

I knew it was going to be hard, but not this hard. I bite my lip and shake my head.

When the bell rings, I hustle out of class before Asha or Emma can catch up to me. I stop in a corner, off the main hallway, and dare to turn on my phone again. I don't open ChitChat, but I check my email. And I have a new message, from Senator Watson's office. I skim it, too scared and upset to even read closely.

Dear Ms. Matthews . . . We appreciate your interest and application to the internship program with Senator Watson. . . . As you are aware, our internship program is highly competitive. . . . We were impressed by your application, but . . . we are not able to offer you a placement at this time. . . .

I stop reading and stuff my phone back in my bag. That's it. It's over. No more internship, likely because the office saw the screenshot, too.

I just can't do it anymore. There is a river running across my skin and the water is closing in over my head. Everything seems completely hopeless.

I've never skipped school before, but now I walk toward the doors to the parking lot and just keep walking. I expect alarms to go off like it's a prison break, but nothing happens.

The parking lot is quieter than I've ever seen it. No screeching tires or loud honks. Every car is neatly in its place and every owner is where they should be—in class.

But not me.

And not Ryan. When I get to my car, he's standing beside it.

I don't know how he knew I would be here now, but something about his solid build standing there, and the look on his face, make me feel some small comfort.

"I'm leaving," I tell him.

"Are you coming back?"

I meet his brown eyes. "Not today." I open the driver's side door.

"What about work?" he asks.

"I'm sick." I get in the car. "I'll call in later."

"Do you want company?" he asks.

I shake my head, wrapping my hands around the steering wheel and staring straight ahead.

He steps into the door opening and leans in. I look up at him.

"It was a brave thing to do," he says.

"Because the screenshot was so awful?" I ask.

"No, because you took your life back. I know that was hard."

"Sometimes brave things really hurt." I start the car.

"That picture doesn't change who you are." He puts his hand on the door to keep me from closing it. His eyes search my face. "Beautiful inside and out," he adds quietly.

I let the words linger between us. It's funny to think that any other day, hearing someone—maybe especially Ryan—call me beautiful might make my heart skip a beat. But today, I'm not sure what to feel anymore.

Still, I can tell he's being truthful. His expression is so earnest. But I can't say anything more.

"Thanks," I tell him, and close the car door.

* * *

The house is empty when I get home. Mom is at work and Megan is at school. Normally, I would get on the computer or my phone. But today is not normal. My world has collapsed.

So I sit on the couch with nothing in my hands, restless for other people's windows to look into—a distraction, a salvation. My brain is working frantically, but I can't see an escape from what I've done. I bury my head in my hands, letting Cassidy nuzzle at my fingers with her soft nose.

When I hear the garage door open, I almost jump out of my skin.

Mom is surprised to find me home and sitting on the couch.

"What are you doing here?" she asks. It's then that I know for sure she hasn't seen the screenshot yet. That's the benefit of having a mom who isn't on social media a lot.

"I didn't feel well. I left school early," I reply.

"What's wrong? Do you have a fever?" She comes over to sit beside me on the couch, putting the back of her hand on my head just like she's done since I was a child. Something about that simple gesture makes me feel better.

"I'm just feeling a little nauseated," I say, and it's kind of the truth. My stomach has felt like a bottomless pit ever since I posted the screenshot.

"You should have called me," Mom says. "I only came home because I forgot my lunch."

I lean against her shoulder and she pushes the hair back from my face.

"I don't have to rush back to work yet," she tells me, and I'm glad. There's a moment of silence, and then Mom adds, "You know, your dad emailed me yesterday."

I'm so surprised I jerk back from her for a minute. "He did?" I honestly can't remember the last time we heard from Dad.

Mom nods, her face a little tight. "It sounds like he's getting his life together more. He got a new job in Texas, finally. He wanted to know if it would be okay if he could call you and Megan up sometime to talk."

I feel myself tighten. "What did you say?" I ask.

Mom hesitates for a minute, then says, "I told him he could." She glances at me. "Is that all right?"

I nod, feeling my tightness start to turn to Jell-O. I've been angry at Dad for a while. We all were—me, Mom, and Megan. But I want to be able to forgive him. Forgiveness is important.

Mom puts her arm around my shoulders and pulls me into a hug. I sink into her side.

"How about some tomato soup? Does that sound good?" she whispers, and then she kisses the top of my head.

"In a minute," I say. "Can we just sit here for now?"

She looks at me carefully. "Sure, sweetie."

After a little while, she pulls away and raises her eyebrows at me. "You want to tell me about it?"

I realize I want that more than anything. I start talking.

CHAPTER SEVENTEEN

SKYE

After I told Mom the whole story, and she listened, and didn't chide me for being careless or irresponsible, and told me she'd be there for me no matter what, I cried a little, and had some tomato soup. And I felt much better. Mom had to go back to work, but she said we'd talk more later.

School was done for the day by then. So I decided there was one thing I needed to do.

I drive to the familiar house, park my car, and get out. I walk around the side and down to the private entrance. This time, I knock on the door and wait for someone to answer.

Asha's eyes widen when she sees me standing there. She steps across the space between us, gathering me into a quick hug.

"I'm so sorry," she murmurs in my ear. My body is stiff and unresponsive, but she doesn't seem to notice. "I tried to catch up with you after class, but you were gone. Did you go home? And you haven't been answering any of my texts! You must be devastated."

How can she be so fake?

Throwing the door open wider, she motions me inside. I sit in the poppy-red chair and she sits across from me on her matching couch. This room has been witness to so much of our lives, but now it feels cold and full of suspicion.

Asha's phone rings from the table on the other side of the room.

"That must be Marcus Lopez," she says. She flashes me a quick smile. "We're kind of dating now, did I not tell you?"

I shake my head.

Asha waves a hand toward her ringing phone. "Just ignore it. This is way more important."

My hands are clamped tightly together in my lap. I wish I could ignore the reality of what's happened. I can't believe I thought Asha was my best friend. Friends don't threaten each other or embarrass each other or blackmail each other.

"Do you want any cookies?" Asha asks. "Mom and I made them yesterday. Chocolate chip? Definitely a cure for a broken heart."

I shake my head again, confused by the random change in topic.

"Asha." I get the conversation back on track. Nothing is going to distract me now that I've made up my mind to confront her. "Why did you want me to do all those things?" I ask.

"What are you talking about?" Asha is a good actress. She looks completely confused.

I try to be cool. *Staycalmstaycalm.*

"The manicure. The dress." My voice breaks and I give a hollow-sounding laugh. "Breaking up with Luke. Are you happy now?"

She leans back against the couch, frowning. "Why would I be happy? I've always liked Luke. It's true I could see how you two weren't totally right for each other. But I didn't want you guys to break up."

She's lying right to my face. I scoot to the edge of the chair and lean in across the space between us. My anger spills out in my voice, but I don't care. It's time for me to stand up for myself. I have to do this.

"Did you send me anonymous messages threatening to share the screenshot of me?" I pull my phone out of my pocket and pull up the ChitChat conversations. I hold the phone out for her to see, my hand shaking. "Look at these, Asha, and then tell me you didn't do it."

Asha takes the phone from my grasp. She reads silently, looks up at me, then back down to read more. A look of shock passes over her face as she scrolls through to the end.

"You thought I did this?" Her face looks ashen, like my accusing her was the worst thing I could have possibly done. "*That's* why you've been so distant lately."

"You were the one who took the video in the first place," I say. "And how do I know you didn't save it to your phone?"

"But I didn't do *this*." She sounds desperate. And hurt. "Skye, listen. I know I can sometimes be pushy . . . and insensitive. But I'd never do anything like this to you. Never."

I want to believe her. Even if it means that then I won't know who is behind the messages. My world is all mixed up in my head.

"Listen, Asha. Sometimes you take things too far and I don't say anything."

"So say something," she says. "Speak up. Tell me. I can take it."

I blink. *Is she serious?*

"I'd rather you tell me what's bothering you than shut me out."

Have I been doing that?

"I feel like I'm *always* in your shadow. You expect me to do whatever you want." Saying the words, I feel a huge relief. And anxiety. I'm saying things I've never said to Asha before. "Maybe what you want isn't always what I want."

"Skye," Asha says, letting out a long breath. "We both know how headstrong I can be, but I never meant for you to feel that way. You are my best friend—and I hope you always will be. I did *not* send you these messages, but when I find out who did . . ."

She clenches her hand into a fist.

"No," I say firmly. It's time to start putting my new-found courage into practice. "This isn't your battle, Asha. It's mine."

Asha nods, and she's quiet for a long moment.

"I haven't been completely honest with you either," Asha finally says. "I couldn't tell you before, but I need to tell someone." She stops, tears filling her eyes.

#IAmAshaMirza *crying*? I'm shocked.

Asha bites her lip and looks down at her hands. Finally, she whispers, "My mom is sick. She has . . . Alzheimer's. She's been sick for a while. And she's not going to get better."

I slip over onto the sofa beside her and wrap my arms around her shoulders. I have so many questions, but it is not the time to ask.

Now is the time to hug.

Asha's tears turn into sobs and I just keep hugging. Honestly, I don't know what else to do.

"I need you to be my friend," Asha manages to get out when she's finally able to speak again. "No matter what happens."

"I'm not going anywhere," I tell her.

We sit together for a while longer. Then my phone buzzes and I reach for it. Asha looks down at the screen, too. A new ChitChat message is waiting there right before our eyes.

TELLTALE♥: I WASN'T GOING TO EVER SHARE THE SCREENSHOT

I grab the phone and immediately write back, fueled by anger.

ME: OH REALLY? WHY WERE YOU TORTURING ME THEN?

In response, I get a photo: a picture of a Band-Aid stuck to a window. And nothing else. I don't know what to make of it.

I look from Asha to the screen and back again. She is sitting right there in front of me. Her phone is across the room.

It hits me then.

It definitely isn't Asha.

CHAPTER EIGHTEEN

SKYE

The next day at work, the checkout lines are long and the aisles are packed with customers. The store seems to be doing better than it has in ages.

I'm actually happy to be here and away from school for a week. The hectic pace of the store keeps me from dwelling on all the events of the past few days. By the time school starts back up, I'm hoping someone else will be the next big thing to talk about. For now, I try to keep from looking online at all. It's the only thing that helps.

Ryan is pushing around the rolling cart with a big pole sticking out of the top. The blue flashing light on top of the rod is off for now, but a small parade of bargain-seekers with overloaded shopping carts still follow him all around the store to be first in line for the next amazing special.

Ryan gives me the go-ahead on the walkie-talkie and I make the announcement from the service desk.

"Attention, Kmart shoppers!" I say. "If you look toward

our hosiery section, you'll see the bubbling blue beacon of bargain . . ."

There is immediately a flurry of activity as the crowd pushes their shopping carts like bumper cars toward the flashing light.

For socks? Seriously?

"There are snacks in the break room," Harmony says, stopping by on her way back to her checkout station. "Millie Johnson made snickerdoodles."

I finish giving a refund for a defective can of spray cheese to a lady who is wearing the signs of splattered cheese all over the front of her purple T-shirt. I nod at Harmony and tell the cheese woman, "Thank you for shopping at Kmart."

Harmony lingers. "Are we getting together tonight after work?" she asks.

I never would have thought it, but our little after-work group has become something I look forward to. For once, there is no expectation to be a certain way. I can just be myself—a different me.

"Yeah," I say. "Ryan said to meet at the Starbucks in Old Town Square."

She smiles, looking happier than I've seen her in a long time. "Cool."

"Did you see the screenshot I posted?" I ask quietly, glancing around for any customers in earshot.

Harmony nods, then shrugs. "You looked hot."

As she walks away to the checkout station, she winks at me. I can't help but smile back.

We drink Starbucks iced lattes and stand listening to a salsa band playing on the stage in the square. The suddenly warm weather has brought everyone out in their flip-flops and shorts, ready to soak in every minute while it lasts. Two little kids are jumping in and out of the fountains, squealing and laughing as the water spurts randomly out of the ground. Over by Ben & Jerry's Ice Cream Shop, a little girl, wearing a very fancy ruffled dress and a big green bow on her head, is in complete meltdown mode. Her father tries to coax her back into a good mood with a spoonful of chocolate chip dangled above her screaming red face, but she is not having it. An elderly couple show off some serious mambo moves in front of the stage, while others simply move to the music—feet tapping and bodies swaying.

It's the perfect spring night—full of possibilities and new beginnings. At the end of our shift, we received good news from Mr. King. Business has improved, so the store will remain open for at least six more months. Now everyone knows what's coming and we have time to try to find new jobs. Harmony has already been successful. She starts working at the gym part time at the end of the month. We're celebrating.

"Congratulations," Ryan says, holding his plastic cup out to Harmony. She taps it with hers.

I touch my cup to the others. "You're going to be great. I'm going to be first in line to sign up for your boxing class."

Harmony grins. "You'd both better be there," she says, nudging Ryan.

We all drink our lattes like they're champagne and we are millionaires—not part-time Kmart employees. A little boy dancing in the fountain misjudges the timing of the water spout and is suddenly drenched in the gush of water. His astonishment results in peals of laughter from the watchers, but a dad quickly rushes in with a warm towel to wrap him up and dry him off. It makes me think of my mom, how good it felt to tell her everything yesterday.

"So what did you say to Asha, after you realized it wasn't her?" Harmony asks me. I've just been filling her and Ryan in on what happened at Asha's place.

"We talked about a lot of things. Stuff I'd been holding on to for a while. Stuff she's been holding on to. She has a lot going on with her family right now that I didn't know about. It felt good to clear the air."

"And how are you feeling about Luke?" Ryan asks.

He looks uncomfortable. "Now that the screenshot is out there, you can try to explain to him more about what happened. You could make it right."

"Maybe," I say. "But I don't want to." I feel like I can finally give voice to something that's been on my mind since possibly the night of the winter prom. "Luke is a wonderful guy, but I was dating him for all the wrong reasons."

"What do you mean?" Harmony asks.

I search for the right words. "I think I was in love with . . . the idea of being with someone as popular as Luke. But that's not the same as being in love with *him*."

Ryan raises an eyebrow.

"I'm okay," I say firmly.

Harmony looks at me doubtfully.

"Seriously, I am. Besides, Luke deserves better," I say.

"So do you," Harmony says. Then she opens her eyes wide and tilts her head toward Ryan, not even trying to be subtle. I feel the heat rush to my cheeks. I give her a dirty look, but she just grins back at me.

I walk ahead of the two of them to let my face cool down. "I do hope Luke and I can be friends again someday," I add over my shoulder. "That's what we're really good at."

"So everything worked out," Ryan says, catching up with me.

"I'm still disappointed about the internship." I swallow

hard, clutching my iced latte. "But I'm determined to volunteer at Senator Warren's office this summer every chance I get and make a good impression."

"With your likability?" Ryan asks, his mouth twitching into a smile.

I shake my head. "With just me—flaws and all."

"But we still don't know who was blackmailing you with the screenshot," Harmony says. She sits down on a metal bench in front of the newly planted flower beds that will be in full bloom by the time the summer tourists arrive.

"Maybe I'll never know," I say, joining Harmony on the bench. I take a sip of my drink and try not to show my drop in spirits.

Ryan sits down on the other side of me and the three of us sit in companionable silence, drinking our lattes.

"Wait," Ryan says, making me jump. "You said the last thing the blackmailer sent you was just a photo?"

I nod, bewildered by his sudden excitement.

"Can I see that picture?" he asks.

"Sure. I have no idea what it means." I fumble in my pocket for my phone and click open to my ChitChat messages. The three of us look down at the close-up of the Band-Aid stuck to the window.

"That's it?" Harmony asks.

I nod.

"Well . . ." She thinks out loud. "I guess Band-Aids are supposed to help things heal? At least it's not some ominous message."

I shrug. It doesn't make any sense. "If this is supposed to be some kind of symbolic peace offering, I'm not taking it."

Ryan hands me his cup to free up both his hands. He takes my phone and taps intently at the screen while Harmony and I watch.

"I thought so," he says.

"What?" I'm confused.

He says, very softly, his voice tight, "There could be a geotag on this photo."

My eyes meet Ryan's. This is important, but I'm not sure why.

"It means the longitude and the latitude of this picture could be stored in the metadata," he explains. "As long as they didn't turn off the location services for their photos." He mumbles the next part almost to himself.

Harmony snorts, then says, "For once I'm glad I don't have one of those fancy phones."

Ryan says, "Yeah, people don't realize how much of your privacy geotagging gives away. You post a photo of something you want to sell online. *Boom*. People can see exactly where it is and can come take it for themselves."

"Why haven't I ever heard of this before?" I ask, surprised.

Ryan shrugs. "It's not super widely known. I only read

about it because I was doing some research on phone cameras."

"So if you post a random photo, a geotag on it could let someone know you're not taking the picture from home?" Harmony asks.

Ryan nods. "Exactly."

"How do you turn it off?" I ask, the iced latte in my hands completely forgotten.

Ryan's eyes are still focused on the screen in front of him. "It's a simple setting switch under location services, but most people don't realize it's there."

"Or how important it is," Harmony says.

I shake my head, trying to understand the implications of what Ryan's telling me. "So you can't tell *who* sent the picture, but . . ."

"I can tell you where it was taken, and if we get lucky, it leads us right to someone's home address." He taps my phone quickly. "There's a free web-based tool where I can upload the photo."

Harmony is leaning over toward Ryan, all big eyes. I just sit and wait, even though I'm not sure what I'm waiting for. There's a long second of silence. Harmony puts a knuckle in her mouth.

Then Ryan says, "Okay. I've found it."

I shut my eyes, terrified of what will come next.

Harmony can't stand it anymore. "What does it say?" she practically yells at him, and my eyes fly open.

Ryan reads off the screen. "The photo was taken with an iPhone yesterday at six thirty p.m."

I'm shocked. My head feels weird and floaty. Instantly, I start trying to think of who was where at six thirty yesterday. "You can tell that by looking at the photo?"

"It's all there in the hidden data stored in the image," he says. "And there's more."

I feel my pulse starting to beat faster.

"When you load the longitude and latitude of the photo into Google Maps, it puts the location . . ." He looks up from his phone, his dark eyes intense. "The photo was taken only a couple of blocks from here."

"Where?" I almost whisper. I feel a chill.

"The Lyric Cinema."

The walls of my world crumble. All this time, I had no idea.

Ryan and Harmony are both watching me.

Harmony finally breaks the silence. "You know." It's not a question.

"Yeah," I say. "I know."

I stand up, taking my phone back from Ryan. I start composing a text.

"Where are you going?" Ryan asks. His voice is concerned.

"I know *who* it is, but now I need to know *why*."

EMMA

FADE IN:

EXT. ASHA'S HOUSE—DAY—LONG SHOT

We see an affluent lakeside community. We
can see the rear of a number of large
houses whose backs are around the lake.
Some are two stories high, some are three;
some have large wraparound decks and
porches. The neighborhood is a prosperous
one. The lake is covered with ice and the
trees surrounding the lake have piles of
snow on their limbs.

THE CAMERA MOVES ACROSS THE LAKE and
brings us nearer to the backyard of ASHA'S
HOUSE. Lights are on in several of the
windows and there are figures moving
around inside the room on the bottom floor.

THE CAMERA IS NOW FOCUSED ON THE SLIDING
GLASS DOORS of ASHA'S ROOM. We are now able

to see inside the room. Loud music is
pouring out of speakers. A short, dark-
haired Indian American girl is standing
facing a closed door. This is ASHA.

THE CAMERA MOVES IN TO FOCUS ON THE DOOR.
The door opens and a pale, brown-haired
white girl with a curvy figure, dressed in
a revealing red nightie, dances out. This
is SKYE. She gracefully moves across the
floor to the rhythm of the music. ASHA
is cheering her on and the second girl is
radiant, twirling and prancing across the
room. They are both laughing.

THE CAMERA NOW PULLS BACK SWIFTLY and
retreats through the sliding glass door
back to the outside of the house. Now there
are hundreds of PEOPLE standing around the
yard and deck of the house, looking in
through the glass.

Emma looks down at the printed and bound script in
her hands. *Her* script. She knows she should be proud.
She should be ecstatic.

The film contest ended thirty minutes ago and

everyone has left the theater. Emma is by herself, sitting near the middle of one long row of seats. She looks like a pale ghost, wrapped in her black overcoat like it's a blanket, her jeans-covered legs and combat boots dangling over the seat in front of her.

The judges were unanimous: Emma's screenplay, a social-media-themed riff on *Rear Window*, won first place. She won the tickets to New York and the applause of the small gathering of judges. *Innovative. Creative. Emotional.*

So why *doesn't* she feel happy?

A text message buzzes onto her phone.

SKYE: I KNOW WHAT YOU DID.

Emma stares at the message with a pit in her stomach. This is the moment she's been dreading since the day after the sleepover. The day she got her idea. She types back as fast as she can.

EMMA: I WAS NEVER GOING TO SHARE IT WITH ANYONE.
SKYE: I NEED TO SEE YOU. NOW.
EMMA: COME TO THE LYRIC.

Emma turns her phone to black and shuts her eyes

tight. If emotion comes directly from a character's eyes, like Hitchcock always said, she'd shoot a close-up right now of the tears that are sliding out her lashes and down her cheek.

But this is real life—and now it's out of her control.

CHAPTER NINETEEN

SKYE

I find Emma sitting in the empty theater. She doesn't look at me when I come through the curtained entrance. Instead, she stares straight ahead, still as a statue. My shoes stick to the floor in spots, and the smell of popcorn still lingers.

I slide into the row and make my way to the seat beside her. The heated air from the wall vents plays at her blonde hair, pulling it out of the low pony and across her face. She drags it back with one hand and tucks the strands firmly behind her ear. Her eyes flick toward me as I sit down, then back to stare at the seat in front of her. I feel her take in a deep breath like she might say something, but then she doesn't.

Since the eighth grade, this is the girl I shared every secret with—the dent I put in my mom's car door when I hit the pole at the Sonic, the first kiss I shared with Ned Blakely behind the gym in middle school, the letter I sent my dad that came back marked "Address Unknown." Something twists in my stomach.

"You sent me the screenshot," I say, trying to keep my voice from wavering. "And all those ChitChat messages. And the picture of the Band-Aid. You're the one who was blackmailing me."

Not one muscle in her beautiful face changes. She says, "Yes, I was."

I knew it was true before I ever came here, but the simply spoken words stab me so deeply I can hardly breathe. The tears gather in my eyes, but I don't try to hide the hurt. I want her to see it. Wet pain streaks down my face. I sit mute, willing her to look at me.

She finally does.

Whatever she sees in my face, it makes her breath catch. There is a long silence. I can hear the street musician out on Mountain Avenue playing the drums and the jingle of the horse's bridle as a carriage pulls away from the square full of laughing kids.

I hold her gaze so she can't look away, and ask the question I've been waiting for so long to know. "Why did you do it?"

It is half a question and half a cry of frustration. Emma bites her lip, looks away, and then sighs. She pulls her feet up over the chair in front of her and wraps her arms around her long legs. For a minute, she rests her forehead on her knees. I wait.

"It was for the screenplay," she mumbles into her knees. After a long time she adds, "I never meant to hurt you."

"I don't understand."

"Neither do I, sometimes. It wasn't supposed to end up like this."

"So tell me," I say, feeling the anger start to rise under my tears.

"In all the years we've been friends, you've never been inside my house, have you?" Emma says, which catches me off guard. I don't answer, so she asks, "Don't you think that's strange?"

What does that have to do with anything right now? I don't know what she's talking about.

"Maybe a little," I say finally.

"There's a reason for that." A muscle in her jaw twitches.

"Emma?" I prod.

"Things at home are . . . not good," she says, her head still down. "My parents . . . fight. All the time. Like, bad fighting. I needed a ticket out. Away from home."

"Oh," I say. My head is spinning. I'm still not sure where all this is going.

"This contest was going to be it," Emma says. "My way out." She looks up at me. Her eyes are the darkest of blues, racing across my face, seeking any sign of forgiveness. I can feel how hard and tight my own features are. "I had to win. I wanted to write the best screenplay, the one that felt the most real. I just got this crazy idea . . . that if I could write the screenplay about something that was happening as it was unfolding, it could be amazing."

I try to take all this in. I shake my head.

"So you . . . used me?" I cut her off. "For some kind of experiment? Some inspiration for a *movie*?"

Emma looks away and nods quickly. "It was just going to be one text, to see how you responded. I know how you hate black nail polish. You said one time it made people look like they had holes in their fingers." She gives a shaky laugh. "I thought you'd tell me to go jump off a cliff when I texted you to choose between the nail polish or the screenshot. You'd say—'go ahead. My picture looks fine. I'm not doing that.'"

"But I didn't." My mouth is dry. There is a wall between us now.

"So I went further." She stops, swallows. "I never thought you'd actually wear that dress to the interview. I knew how much you hated the dress and I knew how much that interview meant. I thought that's when you would call my bluff and tell me no. But the screenshot—that image—was so important that you were willing to do *anything* to keep me from sharing it."

I shudder. "I guess I was."

"And then I was hooked," Emma says.

"And you kept raising the stakes higher and higher."

"Don't you understand? I needed to see what would happen." Emma points to the floor of the theater, where her bound screenplay sits. "The story kept unfolding. And you kept doing what I asked. Even if it meant losing Luke."

I nod, taking that in.

"And even if it meant losing you?" I ask quietly.

She closes her eyes briefly.

"I'm so sorry, Skye. I wanted to tell you. So many times. But . . . I couldn't. I got in too deep. And I was worried you'd never forgive me."

"I don't know if I ever can," I say. The edge in my voice makes her shift in the seat beside me.

"I guess I finally did push you too far," Emma whispers. "Bringing Megan into it was the worst . . . the most horrible . . ."

"Don't even talk about Megan." I blink away tears, my hands clenching into fists. *"Ever."*

"Skye, I don't know how to apologize," Emma murmurs, turning to me. "I thought maybe that picture of the Band-Aid could be a symbol . . . like a way to show we can heal."

I shake my head. How can we heal from this?

Emma frowns. "You have to understand where I was coming from. Please listen. You don't know what living in my house is like . . ." Emma stops talking. A shadow of a bitter smile flickers across her face, then she says, "There's a different story inside people's windows when the shades are pulled down tight. The reality is . . . ugly."

There's a tiny piece of me that hears Emma's pain, that almost feels sad for her, but I'm too focused on my own pain right now. "What do you know about ugly?" I snap.

"You've never looked bad a day in your life. Every angle, every outfit, every photo—beautiful. Your face. Your body. The first thing people think when they look at you is *pretty*."

Emma's face hardens. "You can only see me from your point of view, but you can't walk in my skin. And if you could, you wouldn't like it."

I feel another massive surge of anger, and I stand up shakily. My eyes are stinging and my heart is pounding.

"You're right, I probably wouldn't. And I don't want to look at you anymore either." I stop, breathing hard. "I can't believe I ever thought you were my friend, Emma. One of my *best* friends." I let the words sit there in the air before continuing. "All you are is a bully."

I turn my back on her and walk out of the theater.

EMMA

That night, Emma can't sleep. She sits cross-legged on her bed, clutching her phone in her hand. Like a portal into another world, the screen in front of her has saved her too many times to count. It was her refuge—her life saver.

Now it has betrayed her.

No. Not true.

She was the one who did the betraying. She remembers how upset Skye looked, the things she said in the theater. It breaks her heart. She always loved Skye like a sister. Why *did* she hurt her like that? It wasn't just about the screenplay. It was another way to feel powerful.

She thinks about how Skye will surely tell Asha. How everything will come crashing down. And maybe, in some way, that's what Emma wanted. She had to make a mess of everything before she could truly escape.

Emma dials a familiar number on the phone to make a video call. Summer is still two months away, so all she can do for now is step through the portal and be transported instantly to another life—one she will soon join.

"Hello, sweetie!" her aunt says brightly. "Congrats on winning the contest! Let's make plans . . ."

Her aunt is always so perky. It is something Emma will have to adjust to.

That, and so much more.

CHAPTER TWENTY

SKYE

The first thing I do the next morning is drive to Senator Watson's in-town office. It is located above Cafe Vino and as a result, the waiting room smells like bacon-wrapped dates. A sign taped to the wall says to knock and someone will be with me shortly. I knock, then sit down nervously on the edge of a blue upholstered chair positioned beside the closed office door.

The person who opens the door is immediately recognizable.

I jump to my feet, struggling to find my voice. "Senator Watson."

I'm surprised to see she is only a head taller than me. She looks just as she does in her photos, though, with her big brown eyes, brown skin, and black hair pulled back into a low bun at the nape of her neck. She smiles serenely at me, extending her hand as if I were the leader of some foreign country or a diplomatic emissary. "And you are?"

"Skye . . . Matthews . . . Skye Matthews." I stumble all over the words.

"So nice to meet you in person."

She knows who I am?

"I wanted to come by and ask about volunteering to do . . ." I'm talking so fast, I don't know if anyone could understand me. "Things," I end, lamely.

"Won't you come inside?" Senator Watson gestures for me to enter her office. I walk past her into the room, smoothing my sweater down over my jeans with clammy hands.

What am I going to say?

I sit down in a chair at the cluttered desk, swallowing hard. Senator Watson sits down across from me, brushing back the fallen tendrils of hair behind her ears and still smiling that oh so likable smile. She doesn't have to try to be likable. She just *is*.

"I . . ." Swallowing again, I try to keep my voice from shaking. My tongue feels like it's made of cotton. "I applied to your internship program."

"Yes. I believe I recognize your name. You made quite the impression on James." She sounds amused. "He told me all about your unusual pitch at the interview. You're the one who wore a . . . prom dress?"

I nod, feeling heat engulf my face. "I'm sorry."

"Don't apologize for making a unique space for yourself." Senator Watson tilts her head to one side. "We all agreed it was a very impressive—and memorable—application."

"But I didn't get the internship," I say. Then I screw up

all my courage and ask, "Was it because of my social media photos? That one photo was . . ."

My voice trails off, and Senator Watson shakes her head. "I don't think we reviewed your social media, Skye."

"Oh." I don't know whether to feel relieved or defeated. "You see, there was this not-great picture of me online."

Senator Watson looks at me understandingly. "A lot of us don't always like the way we are portrayed online. I sure don't."

"But you always look so confident." That was going to be next on my to-do list. *Be confident.*

She laughs, her eyes crinkling up at the corners. "Looking and being are two very different things."

I think of Emma, even though I don't want to. "Sometimes there is more to the story than what you see," I admit.

"The internet puts a new spin on the whole appearance thing, doesn't it? It's connecting us in new ways we're just starting to figure out."

"And disconnecting us," I say.

"Exactly." She nods. "We just have to keep trying to be our best selves, even when it seems like everyone is watching and hoping we mess up."

"We're Internauts," I say. "Going where no one has ever gone before."

She looks surprised, then laughs again. "I like that."

"Thanks," I say, blushing. I can't believe I'm being so open with Senator Watson. It feels good.

"If it wasn't the photo, then do you know why I didn't get the position?" I ask.

She pauses, looking directly at me. "I wish we had more paid internships to offer, but it's very competitive. There was another girl who has applied for the past three years. She's worked really hard and we felt it was her time."

I nod. That makes sense. Even though it isn't the outcome I'd hoped for, at least I have some closure now.

Senator Watson stands and holds out her hand. "I hope you'll apply again, Skye. Next year could be *your* time."

After signing up for several upcoming volunteer activities at the senator's office, I leave feeling hopeful. I get into my car, take a deep breath, and then turn on my phone for the first time that morning. Immediately, a string of texts pops up on the screen.

EMMA: I'M SO SO SO SORRY.
EMMA: CAN WE TALK? PLEASE.
EMMA: SKYE? JUST TALK TO ME.

I turn off my phone again. But then I sit there in the parking space with my foot on the brake, staring at the string of silver and gold beads dangling from my rear-view mirror. They catch the sun and shoot light across the dashboard like they are trying to send me some kind of signal. Emma gave the beads to me last New Year's Eve. That night, she put them around my neck just before midnight and then we cheered in the new year—blowing our glittery paper horns and shaking our noisemakers. I blink.

If I look over my shoulder, there will be a black hoodie on the floorboard. Emma keeps it in my car because she always gets cold, even in the middle of summer. There is a book in my backpack I borrowed from her and promised her I'd return, and the earrings I'm wearing are the gold hoops she gave me for my last birthday. I put them on this morning without even thinking about it.

Emma is everywhere.

When my dad left, I tried to shut most people out. If it meant not caring about anyone, then I was determined to spend my life not caring. But Emma had this sneaky little way of squirming right into my hardened heart. She'd meet me halfway between our two houses by the Millers' mailbox. We never actually met the Millers. We never even saw them. But somehow they became a part of our lives. When one of us got there first, we'd just hang out by the big pine tree beside the mailbox and wait for the other. Then we'd hike down to the lake and go paddleboarding. After a while of balancing and drifting, we'd eventually end up just lying on the boards and floating. And talking. About everything and about nothing. Emma called it "paddling it out."

It always made me feel better.

I drive around for half an hour before I finally end up in Emma's driveway. I need to do this face-to-face. No texts. No ChitChats.

When Emma opens the door, her hair is a tangled mess and her face is red and blotchy from crying. She stares at me, uncomprehending. "You came."

Like last night, I almost feel sorry for her. *Almost.*

She steps out onto the porch. "Can we talk out here?"

I nod. We sit on the front step, not close enough to touch, and I wait for her to speak first.

Emma sighs. "Please believe me, Skye. I was never going to actually share the screenshot. I just wanted to see how you would react."

"So I really was some kind of research project?" I cry out, turning to face her. "You can't direct people's lives the way you direct a movie—throwing in a plot twist here or a broken heart there."

"I was going to email you my screenplay. I thought maybe it would help you understand," Emma says. "But when I saw you posted the screenshot, I knew I'd gone too far. I should have told you a long time ago."

I pull my knees into my body and wrap my arms around them tight.

"Have you ever just wanted something so bad, you did a really stupid thing?" Emma asks quietly.

Haven't we all?

"I know you feel like you're always in between Asha and me—in the middle. But Asha is always first." Her voice breaks. "So what does that make me?"

I don't know what to say. My thoughts are whirling.

Her voice is bitter. "The bottom. The last. The worst."

The pain in her voice surprises me more than all the other things she's done. I swallow hard. *Is that how she's felt? All these years? How did I not see this?*

"But you're Emma Middleburg," I argue. "You're gorgeous . . . and talented and . . ." I almost say it, then stop myself. *Perfect is a lie.*

"There are people walking around everywhere who are hiding something they don't want others to know about their lives," Emma says.

I think about Asha and her mother. I think about me and the screenshot. I remember what Emma said, about her parents arguing. I glance behind us, back at her house.

Emma rocks back and forth nervously. "I'm leaving this summer, Skye, and I'm not coming back. At least not for a long time."

I turn back to her, annoyed. "Don't be a drama queen. Of course you'll come back. It's just a trip to New York. This is your home."

"Sometimes home changes. I'm going to go live with my aunt." The words land solidly out into the empty space between us. "There are people in my life I can't help. I can't do *anything* to make other people better, so I have to make me better."

My anger melts just a little. I have to make me better, too.

"I'm sorry. Can you ever forgive me?" Emma's looking at me now, her tears spilling over onto her cheeks. The guilt struggling across her face is terrible. She stands up, her hands hanging loosely by her sides, waiting for me to say something.

A sudden panic makes me want to wrap my arms around her, pushing everything else away. But I'm not there yet. I may be someday soon. It will take some time.

Instead, I stand up and reach out, squeezing her shoulder.

"I don't know," I say honestly. "But I will work on trying."

She nods, wiping her tears with the back of her hand. "I get it. I do. Maybe you could come visit me in New York this summer?"

"Maybe," I say. Then I walk down the porch steps and open my car door. I take out the black sweatshirt from the floor and back seat and hand it to Emma. "Here you go," I add. "In case you get cold in New York."

"Thanks," Emma says, smiling at me through her tears.

I give her a nod and turn away quickly. Then I get in my car and drive off, fighting back my own tears.

After finishing her last day of work at Kmart, Harmony steps off the bus in Old Town with a smile still lingering. She looks down at the photos Ryan just posted on ChitChat, all tagged #wellmissyouharmony. She'd never had a party thrown in her honor before.

She thinks for a moment about checking in at the gas station and maybe saying hello to Matthew, but decides she can do without her usual Diet Coke and doughnuts for today. Besides, she's still full from Millie Johnson's three-tiered cake, red velvet with cream cheese frosting—her favorite. It was the hit of the break room.

Suddenly, an email dings onto her phone. She opens it and starts to read.

> **Thank you for your interest in a Habitat Home. . . . We here at Habitat for Humanity believe everyone should be able to have a safe and affordable place to call home. . . . Your application was exceptional. . . . We are very happy to inform you of our decision to select your family as the next Habitat homeowners in Fort Collins. . . .**

Harmony gets to the end of the email, then reads it again, stopped full in the middle of the sidewalk and oblivious to the people grumbling around her as they try to avoid running into her. Finally, she raises her head and closes her eyes, face up to the sky, taking it all in. For a long minute, she stays like that, letting the crowd stream around her.

Days later, when Harmony has settled into her bedroom—her new bedroom, that she will share with her mom—the first thing she does is sit down on the edge of her bed and take her phone out of her pocket. She logs on to ChitChat and types a message for the whole Galactic Network to see.

HARMONY CHECKED IN AT *HOME*.

CHAPTER TWENTY-ONE

SKYE

That night, the doorbell rings, and it's Ryan. When we were working the morning shift earlier, we made plans to watch a movie at my place.

He walks in wearing jeans, a red T-shirt, and a black hoodie, and he's carrying a tinfoil-covered pan. My face instantly feels hot, which is silly since I just saw him earlier today. He looks so good standing there, running a hand through his dark, spiky hair. My heart beats a little faster.

He hands me the pan while dodging Cassidy's enthusiastic greeting. "My grandmother made *taisan*. It's like a Filipino chiffon cake. Topped with melted butter and sugar."

"Yum. Thanks. We can have some after the movie." I take it from him and walk into the kitchen, putting it up on the top of the fridge so Megan won't find it first. "How's your grandmother doing?" I ask when I rejoin Ryan in the living room.

"Better. She's moved from Elvis songs to Dolly Parton. Always a good sign."

I smile. "And the ghost?"

He shrugs, and the corners of his mouth turn up. "Still there as far as I know."

We sit down on the couch. I start to reach for the remote, but Ryan clears his throat, looking nervous. I start to feel nervous, too.

"What is it?" I ask him.

"I have something else for you," he says. He pulls out a red shiny package with a bright yellow bow on top from the pocket of his hoodie.

"For me?" My mouth falls open. "But it's not my birthday or anything."

"Don't worry. It's just a little something I thought you might like," he says.

I glance up at Ryan and see a smile in his eyes, but I also see something else. There is something in those brown depths that makes my heart thump. It feels like a fresh start.

Sparks. Tingles. Possibilities.

Slowly, I unwrap the present, tearing away the glittery paper. Inside is a small silver frame that contains a photo of me. It's a picture Ryan took on the day we went snowshoeing, but I don't remember posing for it. I'm caught unaware, not trying to impress anyone. I'm kneeling on the snow and Cassidy is wrapped in my arms. We are both smiling happily, but only one of us has a tongue hanging out of her mouth.

While I'm still looking at the photo, Ryan says, "I have a confession to make."

I glance up, confused. "What?"

Ryan doesn't meet my eyes. "I was really proud of this picture, and I wanted to show it to you . . . but with all the screenshot stuff happening, I didn't know how you'd feel."

"I understand," I say. "But it's not like you shared it online."

Ryan shakes his head. "I did show it to Harmony, though. I wanted her opinion. But that's all." He swallows. "I wanted to be sure you'd like it."

My heart swells. "I love it," I say. I glance back down at the picture. "It's beautiful."

"Like you."

I look back up at Ryan. The first time he told me I was beautiful, I was too upset to even process it. Now I hear him. Ryan meets my eyes and I catch my breath. The air is so sparky between us I feel it could catch fire at any moment.

I can't look away. He's so close. It leaves me feeling light-headed. There is something between us that is new and fizzy and oh so appealing. The best part? I can tell he feels it, too.

I nibble on my lower lip nervously and Ryan's gaze drops from my eyes to my mouth. Then I surprise us both by doing something I've always been afraid to do before—I make the first move. Leaning in, I kiss him full on the lips. Soft. Tentative. When I pull away, I can see the surprise on his face. My head feels buzzy and I can hardly breathe. I feel the color flush up in my cheeks.

What happens now?

"I've been imagining that kiss for a very long time," Ryan whispers, and I realize I have, too. He cups my face with his hands, his eyes roaming my face. Every nerve in my body is tingling.

He finds my mouth and kisses me again. I melt into his body.

This feels so different from when Luke and I would kiss. But different in a good way. In the best way.

"Hello?" Megan is standing in the middle of the living room with her hands on her hips. "Are we going to watch a movie or are you guys going to just make out?"

I jerk away, heat rushing into my face, but Ryan just laughs. He gives me an additional quick kiss on my lips for emphasis, even though Megan is still standing right there in front of us.

"Come on, Megan. Give a guy a break." He grins, leaning back against the cushions of the couch. He keeps one arm firmly around my shoulders. "You get the popcorn and we'll start the movie, okay? What do you want to watch?"

She rolls her eyes and stomps off toward the kitchen. "Definitely not a romance."

My mom comes into the living room then, wrapping a bright-blue scarf around her neck. Mom has met Ryan before when she's picked me up at the store, and she greets him with a warm smile.

She's wearing a beige cabled sweater dress that hits just at the top of her coffee-colored Frye boots. Her hair is softly curled around her shoulders and she has on pink lipstick that I've never seen her wear before.

"How do I look?" she asks nervously, and gives a small twirl for our benefit.

"Great," I say, and she does. It's hard to believe she's going out on a date, but I can see how happy it makes her. It's funny, but she didn't meet this guy on the internet. It all happened the old-fashioned way. They met at Alleycat when he made her latte and they started talking. Totally old school.

"We're just meeting at the coffee shop," she says. "Mike's not even picking me up or anything."

"I get it, Mom. It's totally casual," I say. "Have fun."

She gives Megan a quick hug, then waves good-bye to me and Ryan. Megan goes into the kitchen, Cassidy following along behind, and I can hear the microwave start up. In minutes there is popping and the smell of fresh popcorn.

I lean my head on Ryan's shoulder, thrilled by how comfortable I feel with him. I pick up the remote and turn on Netflix, flipping through the options.

"How about a comedy?" Ryan says.

"I don't know," I reply. "I think I'm in the mood for action. Maybe even superheroes."

Ryan grins. "Cool. Wait, I texted you some suggestions earlier. Did you see them?"

"Nope. My phone is upstairs."

Ryan's eyebrows rise. "Do you want to go get it?"

I shake my head. "I'm good without it. I'm thinking maybe I need a bit of a break from the whole Galactic Network thing. Besides, I'll never be here again in this moment in time. I don't want to miss anything."

"Interesting." He pulls his phone out of his pocket and turns it off. "Hey, Megan," he calls.

She pops her head out of the kitchen. "What?"

"Can you put this in the pantry for me?" He holds out his phone over the back of the couch.

"Okay . . ." Megan walks over and takes it from him. "Why?" she asks, confused.

"We're playing a game." He smiles at her. "No phones allowed."

"Can I play?"

"Absolutely," he says, and Megan happily goes back to the kitchen to supervise the popcorn.

Ryan turns to me. "Should we discuss *Democracy in America*? I actually finished the book," he says proudly.

"I'm impressed."

"Or better yet, why don't you tell me what you volunteered to do at Senator Watson's office."

"So you're saying we should just . . . talk?" I laugh.

He nods. "Exactly."

I risk a sideways look at Ryan. He's smiling. I lean my head back on his shoulder. He takes my hand in his and slips it deep into the warmth of his sweatshirt pocket. Our fingers intertwine.

Megan comes back from the kitchen, dropping kernels of popcorn along the way like bread crumbs from Hansel and Gretel. Cassidy happily cleans up after her. Megan sits down on the couch, hands me the big bowl of popcorn, and I snuggle closer into Ryan.

"What are we talking about?" she asks.

"Changing the world," I say.

TO DO:
PUT YOUR PHONE AWAY
~~SHOW EMPATHY. SAY, "ME TOO."~~
~~MAKE EYE CONTACT~~
~~LEAD CONVERSATIONS WITH A COMPLIMENT~~
~~SMILE MORE~~

ACKNOWLEDGMENTS

For every life window posted on any screen, there is always more to the story. This book was inspired by those stories and the hope we can recognize the truth behind the screenshots with empathy and kindness.

First, thank YOU for reading. No book is complete without a reader.

Special appreciation to my agent, Sarah Davies at Greenhouse Literary, who watches over my literary world with brilliant attention and expertise.

Thank you to my editor, Aimee Friedman, whose editorial direction and support have changed my writing and my life. Thanks to my Scholastic dream team of experts who bring each book to life and then deliver them to the hands of readers with amazing care—especially David Levithan, Tracy Van Straaten, Rachel Feld, Isa Caban, Olivia Valcarce, Yaffa Jaskoll, Rachel Gluckstern, Kerianne Okie, Maria Chang, Jessica White, Rebekah Wallin, the entire Sales team, everyone in the Clubs and Fairs, and so many more.

Thanks to my writing friends, who make me laugh and lift me out of the depths of creative angst. I am so amazed by their inspired talent and kind support: Veronica Rossi, Talia Vance, Bret Ballou, Kathi Appelt, Debbie Leland, Beth Hull, Robin Fitzimmons Meng, and Kristen Held. Special gratitude to Katherine Longshore for her early reading and thoughtful editorial feedback. Much appreciation also to my work colleagues and friends who support this crazy writing dream—especially Karmen Kelly, Karen and Greg Rattenborg, and Wendy Fothergill.

Thanks to my family for being my first readers and biggest supporters. I love you all so much and am so incredibly blessed by your encouragement and unconditional love.

Thank you to my husband, Jay—my travel companion, my adventure partner, my fierce protector, my best friend, and my love—for sharing your Filipino culture with this story and for answering many questions along the way. *Mahal na mahal kita.* You make my creative life possible.

Miss you, Mom. Every. Day.

POINT PAPERBACKS
THIS IS YOUR LIFE IN FICTION

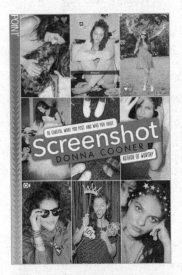

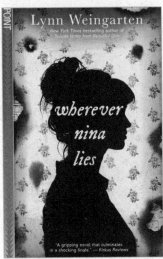

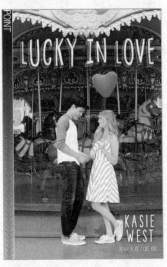

BOOKS ABOUT LIFE. BOOKS ABOUT LOVE.
BOOKS ABOUT YOU.